A Little Bit Psychic

By Aimée Avery

Ave

ISBN-10: 1-4421-4003-8
ISBN-13: 978-1-4421-4003-5

A LITTLE BIT PSYCHIC

First Printing 2009

Printed in the U.S.A.

Contact the author by e-mail at:
ThePemberleyCafe@gmail.com

In Memory of
Linda Mobray-McCain
~ Your heart beat true, and so will your memory ~
&
Mary Stelma Ostrand
~ May you always show off your Dandies ~

~ For Jane ~

~ Special thanks to ~

Stevie, my Cabana Boy, for putting up with my hobby.

Dana, Debra and AmyJ for finding my errors. Let's hope I caught them all.

And to all my readers and friends at
Hyacinth Gardens and Austen Underground.

Chapter 1

"Charlotte! Must you tell everyone?" Elizabeth Bennet asked her friend visiting from the United States.

"Oh, come on, Liz! It isn't like I'm telling any state secrets or anything." Charlotte smiled at her and then turned back to Liz's mates. "Ever since I can remember, she'd have these dreams and, sure enough, every one came true."

"Is she telling the truth, Elizabeth?" Margaret Martindale asked. "If she is, why in the world would you choose to study English Literature? I would think you'd want to do your thesis on something more, oh, I don't know... The hidden powers of the brain?"

"I would love to be a little bit psychic," Sally McKendrick mumbled.

"I am not psychic. For Pete's sake!" Elizabeth exclaimed just before she gulped down the rest of her Strongbow. "I need another pint!"

As Elizabeth rose from her seat to venture back to the bar for a refill, Charlotte whispered to the others, "She has always been a bit touchy over the subject. The popular girls in our class used to ask her to tell their fortunes, and when she couldn't do it, they would be quite mean. Her talents don't come on demand."

"I think it's very interesting," Margaret said as she sat straighter. "I have the greatest respect for Elizabeth, and would never treat her badly.

I'd like to talk to her more about this."

"Is that why she decided to work for her PhD in England, instead of the States?" Sally enquired.

"I think her mother was the deciding factor in that," Charlotte said between sips. "Mrs. Bennet is a nice woman, just... well, she's a bit much. If you know what I mean."

Elizabeth returned to the table, put her drink down and sat hard in her chair. She looked around at each of the faces and felt guilty for snapping. She wasn't sixteen anymore, and this wasn't Longbourn High School. She was twenty-five, had a master's degree in literature, and was actively working toward her PhD at the University of Greenwich.

She was lucky to have obtained a room in Devonport House, just across from the campus. She hoped to meet other postgraduate students, and maybe find a flat they could all share. Though the refurbished historic building was specifically for mature students in the postgraduate program, the £95 per week was a steep price for the small space. With such prices, she had to take a job tutoring to help finance her studies, thus turning her two-year program into four. Consequently, she hadn't been able to befriend many postgraduate students. Instead she had befriended a few of the undergraduates she had been tutoring, and had just moved from the small space at Devonport House into a flat with three second-year Greenwich students.

Now, after a year in London, Elizabeth was glad that Charlotte Lucas had come to visit; even if she deemed it necessary to tell her new flatmates about her prescient dreams.

"Elizabeth, please tell us more about this phenomenon," Margaret suggested. "Not that this falls within the realm of my course of study, but I find all things to do with the brain fascinating. I'm positive that our brains have many powers we don't understand or even use."

"Thank you, Margaret." Lizzy smiled. "I've spent a good deal of my childhood as the object of ridicule over this. I'm sorry to be so touchy."

"No. No, I understand," Margaret waved off her apology. "This is something I would like to research. Perhaps after I transfer, I can devote more time to it, but right now, I would like to hear about your experiences. Would you tell us? Please?"

Elizabeth looked at Charlotte, who shrugged then smiled, and pulled in a deep breath and started her story.

"Well, the first time I remember having one of these dreams and realizing they were coming true was when I was five..." Elizabeth explained how her father took the family to a summer retreat sponsored by his employer. It was at a lake that had large, modern cabins and an activities director to keep the children entertained while the adults relaxed. One rainy afternoon, the storms had been strong enough to knock out the electricity, and the children sat in the main cabin, listening to a story about a knight on a horse who saved the princess from an evil lord who wanted to be king.

"My sister, Jane, who was seven at the time, and I argued over whether there were such things as knights who would save damsels in distress. She insisted that there might have once been knights who did such things, but not anymore. I, of course, disagreed. She huffed and left me to go play with some other girls who, like her, all had a crush on a boy named Will. I was upset at being abandoned and being told I was a baby for believing in stories, so I shot out of the cabin as soon as the rain stopped and ran into the woods.

"I had followed some of the boys through the woods, and knew about their 'secret cave' hideout, so I went there and played until I fell asleep. That's when I had my first experience. I remember thinking that this wasn't like a normal dream."

Elizabeth explained how her young mind perceived the difference to a normal dream, then went on to tell them of the dream itself.

"I was in the cave and looked out to see that it was nearly dusk. I was very scared, and not sure I could find my way back in the dark. Then I saw a light flash into the cave, and thought it my knight come to save me. My knight came in and took my hand and led me back and my sister. Jane stomped her foot because I had this very pretty princess dress on; not to mention that the knight was the ten year-old boy that she had a big crush on.

"Well, I woke up with a smile, until I looked out of the cave and realized that it was dark like in my dream. And with the exception of the dress, my dream came true. The boy my sister had a crush on did find me and take me back."

"Wow, that's so cool," Sally giggled.

"I still have the dreams, and they are never anything more than trivial bits, but they all start with a whistling sound and look as if I am looking at the future through a window."

"I dreamed that Charlotte was going to get skates for her birthday, and about my youngest sister getting pregnant, then married to the bum she slept with. I also dreamed about Jane getting engaged, which she did. Things like that."

"How often do you have the dreams?" Margaret asked.

"There is no regularity to them. And I'm not always asleep when I have them."

"How do you dream if you aren't asleep?" Sally asked.

"Well, it's more like a daydream, Sally. But that rarely happens. My mind has to be blank, and I'm afraid that doesn't occur very often." Elizabeth laughed.

"Yeah, Liz. You really do think too much," Charlotte laughed.

"Oh, hey! Here comes Mary!" Sally exclaimed as she rose and waved her hand frantically so the newcomer would spot the group.

"Charlotte, meet Mary King. Mary, this is my friend from home, Charlotte Lucas," Elizabeth introduced them.

The two women exchanged greetings before Mary pulled a magazine from her messenger bag.

"Look what I bought on my way to the Tube," Mary pointed to the magazine.

"Whoa! Who's the looker?" Charlotte asked.

"Oh my God! William Darcy! That man is so yummy!" Sally drooled over the glossy photo gracing the magazine cover.

Elizabeth started at the name, and looked at the magazine. It was a moment or two before she realized that the three women were staring at her. "What?"

"You zoned," Charlotte said. "What did you see?"

"What are you talking about?" Elizabeth quickly brought her glass to her lips.

"Lizzy, you had one. What did you see?"

"Had one what?" Mary asked.

"You had one of those dreams, didn't you?" Margaret asked.

"What dreams?" Mary looked back and forth between the women.

"Oh, Elizabeth is just a little bit psychic, and she saw something. And we want to know what!"

Elizabeth swallowed hard and wondered how she was going to

explain that she just had her first "psychic" sex dream.

Chapter 2

"I really like your flatmates, Lizzy," Charlotte said as she settled on the air mattress in Elizabeth's room. "They all seem nice, though I'm not too sure about Mary."

"She's just young, Char. I think this is her first time living away from home."

"Maybe," Charlotte offered as she stared into the darkness after switching off the light. "So, tell me about your 'vision,' and none of that crap about seeing a stupid antique bed in your bedroom that isn't your bedroom."

Elizabeth had stumbled just enough when explaining her psychic vision that Charlotte knew there was more than the description of the antique four poster she had seen in some consignment shop in a bedroom that was Lizzy's, but not the one they were in now. Luckily, her new flatmates didn't know her well enough yet to discern the deception.

"Spill, girl!"

"Um, well, I'm not sure I can, Charlotte."

"Lizzy! Come on! We've been friends forever. There is nothing you can't tell me,"

"It's sort of... well, embarrassing," Lizzy winced.

"Ohhhhkay. Go on."

"Oh, all right! But don't you dare tell anyone. And I mean anyone!"

"Fine. I won't tell anyone. Do you need me to draw some blood too?"

"Ugh! Okay, okay." Though happy the lights were out in the room, Elizabeth couldn't help but cover her face with the blanket to hide from her embarrassment.

"Well, the four poster that I have been salivating over was in the dream, or at least a similar piece. And it was in a room that I know was my bedroom, but it was huge, and I have never seen it before. All my things were there and..."

"And what, Lizzy?"

"And there was someone else there with me." Lizzy's voice squeaked in discomfort.

"Who?"

"Oh, God!" Elizabeth mumbled. "It was... was... W-Will Darcy."

"The guy on the magazine?" Charlotte sat up and stared at where she remembered Lizzy to have been when the room was illuminated.

"Yes."

"Boy, your roomies are going to be jealous!"

"Charlotte! You can't say anything! I had no idea the Will Darcy I knew as a kid was Britain's juiciest bachelor now!"

"As a kid? Is he the knight-in-shining-armor Will?"

"Yeah. And someone I haven't seen in many, many years, so..."

"Okay. I get it. So you don't want them knowing you used to know the guy."

"Right."

"Fine. My lips are sealed. But what the heck was he doing in your bedroom in your vision?"

"This is the embarrassing part. We... We were having s... having sex."

"W-What?" Charlotte laughed while Elizabeth buried her head under her pillow and moaned. "Oh, you have to tell me now! If you think I'm going to let you stop now, you're nuts!"

Elizabeth closed her eyes and recalled the dream. She always remembered her visions with photographic accuracy and, what initially zipped through her mind in just a couple of seconds, was remembered in real time. As she aged, it seemed as if her "dreams" were more than just pictures, but experiences felt as well as visualized.

"I have no idea of where or when, but I do know that the bedroom we're in is mine, as is the bed. I mean, I haven't even seen this guy since I was fifteen. I've been here a year, and haven't seen him. It is possible he knows I'm here in the UK. My dad does work for Darcy Corp."

"But how is it that you are having sex?"

"I don't know, Char!"

"Describe the sex part." Charlotte commanded. "Exactly. Inquiring minds need to know."

"I feel like I went to a porn movie."

"Whoa! Okay, keep talking!" Char chuckled.

"Well, the dream started with me realizing the room and the bed. Then I realized that I was naked and up on my knees. I was looking up at the ceiling, and the next thing I realized was... Oh, this is so embarrassing!"

"I get that, Lizzy! But you know you have to tell me, so just pretend you are describing one of those scenes from those hot romance novels we used to palm from your mom."

"Right." Elizabeth blew out a breath and knew she would feel better telling someone about this particular dream. She would walk around for the next four weeks a nervous wreck if she didn't. Charlotte may like to tell people she had "visions," but if there was one thing Lizzy knew, it was that Charlotte wouldn't reveal the content of any dream told to her.

"Well, I'm up on my knees because I am straddling him. He is underneath me and... and... and inside me..."

"Oh, good Lord! Whew. Who needs a trashy novel when there are your dreams, girl!"

"Charlotte!"

"Sorry. Go on."

Elizabeth continued as she ignored the moans and groans of jealous pleasure Charlotte let out. Elizabeth closed her eyes and placed herself inside her mind. In a calm and composed voice, she described the vision.

"We're on the bed. I'm on my knees, naked and straddling him.

He's inside me and, oh, does it feel wonderful. Full and tight. My breasts tingle and I look down at them. He is sitting up and is pinching my right breast with his fingers and sucking on my left. He says that I taste good. Then all of a sudden he's grabbed a hold of my legs, and is lifting me so he can lay me down. But he doesn't allow me to go all the way back on the bed. He's holding me in such a way that he can get up on his knees, and the way it all feels makes me come like a volcano. Then I am on my back, and he is pounding into me and my legs are wrapped around him. I know he is about to come, and that is when you started calling to me and snapped me out of it."

"Remind me to never call to you when you are in a trance."

❦ ❦ ❦

Elizabeth enjoyed Charlotte's visit, even with her constant teasing over her "sex" dream. She was only too happy that Charlotte managed to keep her jabs either cryptic or executed only when they were alone. And after three weeks of showing her friend around London, Elizabeth escorted Charlotte to Heathrow by way of London's public transportation systems.

Charlotte, of course, managed to get in as many references to what she now called Elizabeth's sex dream man or "SDM" in the hour or so the duo spent on the DLR, Jubilee and Piccadilly Lines. As much Elizabeth loved her friend, she was almost happy to see her leave.

Lizzy spent the ride back to her flat listening to an audio book on her iPod. By the time she boarded the DLR back to Greenwich, the audio book had been abandoned, and her nerves were just as itchy as when Charlotte was teasing her. It seemed William Darcy was very popular tabloid news, and everyone on the Tube seemed to have a newsprint or magazine version of his face handy to stare at her. Elizabeth hoped the press was as fickle as her sister, Lydia, and as time passed, so would the focus of the subject the tabloids chose to concentrate on.

Elizabeth sat on the train and remembered the last time she saw William Darcy. She was fifteen. It had been ten years after he rescued her. Jane's crush on him had ended in favor of fairer-haired boys, and Elizabeth's had silently taken over. But, at fifteen, she was still tomboyish enough not to care about party dresses and makeup. She preferred to run about the lake playing volleyball and canoeing. Will hadn't come to the summer retreats the three previous years. He'd been away at university. The now twenty year-old man came Lizzy's fifteenth year to aid his recently widowed father. He also brought his girlfriend; his very feminine, model-esque girlfriend, Caroline Younge.

Elizabeth hated the woman on sight. Not only was she tall and beautiful, she looked good no matter what she wore. From an elegant summer shift dress to old cut-off shorts and a ragged T-shirt, Caroline Younge looked fabulous. Elizabeth felt short and plain around the woman, and therefore, fell back on what she could do. In all her girl-ish enthusiasm, Lizzy tried to show off her talents for sports and impress the boy turned man. But William saw her only has a child who could use her lack of height to infiltrate the front line and foil the opposing teams attempt to spike the ball.

What made it even worse was the afternoon before the summer finale, a party to celebrate the end of the summer fun, Elizabeth man-aged to secure Will's promise that he would dance at least one dance with her. Lizzy was nervous enough without her sisters making fun of the fact she was to actually wear a dress, that she needed to escape the cabin and the company of a ten, twelve and thirteen year-old follow-ing her about with their jeers. Jane's wise seventeen years managed to corral the younger girls while Elizabeth slipped out and walked into the woods where she had once been the damsel in distress.

There was a tree near the spot where Will had "rescued" her she liked to climb and look out over the lake. As she stood and looked at the tree, she had her first dream of dread, and knew this would be the last summer retreat in a very long time, if forever. Though she could not see what was to happen, it was to be something sad, and important enough to end these beautiful summers, and she felt the need to climb the tree and take that one final look about the lake and make it a per-manent memory.

Sitting on a high branch with the wind teasing her face, Elizabeth heard a woman's laugh, followed by a man's just below her. Turning to look down at the intruders, she watched as Will Darcy pushed Caroline up against the tree trunk and kissed her passionately. Lizzy watched as her heart shattered. Tears began to stream down her cheeks as she listened to the conversation exchanged between the lovers on the ground below.

"I wish we thought to bring a blanket," Caroline spoke as she pulled at Will's shirt.

"We don't need a blanket."

"William! I am not going to do it in the dirt."

"Hmm, getting dirty sounds quite nice," Will's voice was husky.

Caroline chuckled before saying, "Yes, but everyone will know, and your father already is disapproving enough."

Elizabeth was happy that George Darcy wasn't very fond of his son's girlfriend. It was obvious to even her that Caroline Younge liked Will more for his money than anything else. Well, maybe she liked this part too, except for the getting dirty.

"Besides, Will, I'm not like that little girl that follows you everywhere."

"What are you talking about?" William asked as he pulled back from Caroline to look at her.

"Your little Miss Eliza. You do know she has a crush on you?" Elizabeth felt dizzy and quickly hugged the tree to keep from falling.

"The Princess?" Will laughed. "Lizzy is just a child! She is more interested in learning to Jet Ski than boys, let alone have a crush on someone who is more or less a brother figure."

Caroline gave him a look as if he had to be a dense fool. "William, she begged you to dance with her at the party tonight. I know the female mind, and she has a crush on you; not to mention the little bitch has tried to sabotage me with your father!"

The ringing of Will's mobile phone interrupted the conversation, and the two left the woods hand in hand. Elizabeth managed to shimmy down the tree and make it back to the cabin, where she claimed not to feel well. She never made it to the party that evening, and the Bennets left for home early the next morning. Three week's later, George Darcy suffered a non-fatal heart attack, putting an end to the family summer retreats the company sponsored. Corporate expansion was emphasized instead of family retreats, and Elizabeth Bennet decided that white knights no longer existed.

Lizzy returned to the flat and resumed her studies with fervor. She also continued tutoring, and six months managed to slip by without notice, as did any remnants of her psychic sex daydream or summer retreat memories. Margaret Martindale transferred to Avery Hill, and a friend of Mary King's took up the vacancy in the flat. All seemed well until Elizabeth awoke one morning with a feeling of dread. Something was about to happen, but she could not see or feel what it was. But whatever was to come, was making her nerves itchy, just as Charlotte's teasing had done, and Lizzy knew that this dreaded happening was going to take her down a path leading directly to William Darcy.

Chapter 3

William sat at an outside table with his cousin, Richard Fitzwilliam, and hoped the throng of tourists eating at this pub didn't trip over themselves and dump their drinks all over him.

"This pub seems a bit popular with the tourists. Why did you choose to meet here, Richard?"

"I didn't. Caroline suggested it," Richard smiled and nodded toward the entrance to the patio. "Speak of the devil. Or should I say she-devil?"

"Watch your mouth, Richard!" Caroline sashayed up to the table and slapped his arm as the two men rose. She leaned and kissed Richard's cheek as Darcy spoke.

"I believe she prefers "witch" to "she-devil." Darcy's voice was full of amusement.

"You watch it too, mister!" Caroline snapped and then kissed William's cheek. "The two of you are too cheeky for your own good. I'm going to have to do something about that."

Richard's head snapped up, and he quickly looked between his two companions. "You'd better not do the same thing to Will that you'll do to me!"

"I'm sure Caroline will have something much better worked up for me than you, Richard." Darcy said with a smile and a wink to Caroline, then let out a laugh when Richard's eyes seem to slip from their sockets."Stop teasing him, William. He still hasn't recovered from that summer I went with you to the States," Caroline chastised.

"Yes, Will! Caroline is my wife! Stop making the moves on her!" Richard growled.

"Calm down, cousin. I am not making the moves on your wife! She's not my type anyway."

"Okay, you two. Stop with the male struggle for dominance. You are the one I want, Richard. Always you. Just you."

"Except for that summer," Richard muttered dejectedly.

"No, Richard. Not even then. Not that I didn't try my best," William said kindly. That summer had been a hard one on William. His mother had passed away just months before. The retreat was something his mother planned every year, and it seemed wrong not to continue with it after all the work she had put into it. He promised his father he would attend. His younger sister, Georgiana, was only eleven, and the loss of her mother affected her acutely. She seemed to slip further within herself. The only time she seemed to enliven was when her older brother was present.

He hadn't attended the retreats for the three years previous to that last one. He thought it best under the circumstances. After the lecture his father had given him the summer before he entered university, it seemed best. But that last year, his father almost begged him to come for his sister's sake. He thought it might be prudent if he took along Caroline. She had recently broken up with Richard, and they thought it would be mutually soothing if they struck up a fancy for each other. Only George Darcy could see past the show, and he wasn't too fond of the pairing.

"I'm sure you did!" Richard scowled.

"Richard. William and I never did anything. Yes, he tried, but neither one of us really wanted the other. I wanted you, and William here wanted his princess," Caroline explained to her husband.

"I believed you when you said that you two never, um, well, got it on. But what is this 'princess' business? Neither of you has ever mentioned this before." Richard Fitzwilliam was intrigued. His cousin never seemed to stay in a relationship more than a few dates. Could this "princess" be the reason?

"It isn't something I like to talk about," William said.

"Darcy! I'm your cousin. Your blood. My wife knows, but I don't! Now that makes me suspicious!" It didn't really, but Richard wasn't about to let his cousin slide on this tidbit.

William sat for a moment and fingered the condensation on his drink glass. Without looking up, he began to speak. "You remember the story where the little girl was lost in the wood?"

"Yes. The one you found? You were, what? Ten?"

"Yes. Elizabeth Bennet was five. She dubbed me her 'knight' for saving her; she was the damsel in distress. I called her 'Princess' after that. Every summer, she would follow me around. It bothered me a little at first. After all, when you're twelve, the last thing you want is a seven year-old girl following you about. But I just began to expect it. When I was seventeen, she was twelve and..."

"Okay, so I get you're five years older, so what does that have to do with the rising price of crude oil?" Richard asked before his wife could get her hand on his arm to belay the comment.

Darcy looked up at his cousin with shame and sadness in his eyes. Richard sat, almost stunned at the expression on his cousin's face.

"That summer, I realized that the Princess was growing up. She always liked to swim in the lake, and that year she wore her older sister's hand-me-down bikini. Only Lizzy, at twelve, filled out the bikini better than Jane ever did. Her body had blossomed into a woman's, but she was still a kid. But that didn't stop me... um, wanting her."

Richard seemed a bit shocked, and then realized that his cousin, even at seventeen, would never do anything foolish.

"No one seemed to notice that I looked at her that way, or so I thought."

"Uh oh!" Richard mumbled. "What happened?"

"Both Mr. Bennet and my father noticed. Neither was pleased. I would never have done anything, but I couldn't help looking. I was just a kid myself. My father took me aside and spoke to me. I have never been so embarrassed in my life. I managed to finish out that summer, but decided not to attend the retreats anymore; not until mother died and father begged me to go for Georgie's sake. You and Caroline had broken up, and I thought if she went with me, she could distract me."

"Only it didn't work," Caroline added in. "Now he was twenty and she was fifteen, and a beauty if I do say so myself. William kept himself in check, but he would have to get away from her after a while. That's when he tried to hit on me. But I knew he wanted little Eliza. Funny thing was, his little princess had the hots for him too. She even begged him to dance with her."

"Really now?" Richard smiled.

"The night you came to claim your girlfriend, there was a dance. She had asked me earlier in the day if I would dance with her. I waited for her, but she never showed. Apparently she wasn't feeling well."

"You never told me that!" Caroline exclaimed with surprise.

"I don't think she was as infatuated as you thought." William smiled. "I haven't seen her since. I was invited to her high school and college graduations, but didn't attend. My father did go to the first, and took her the gift I bought for her, but..."

"I suppose she is married with two point five children now?" Richard said before he took a drink from his glass.

"No. She is here in London, studying for her PhD," William added casually.

"And you haven't seen her?" Mr. and Mrs. Fitzwilliam asked in unison.

William chuckled. "No. I haven't. Though she does visit with Mr. Reynolds and his wife every so often. They keep me apprised."

"Well, I, for one, think you should look her up. After you barked at me that day for saying she was trying to incite problems between your father and me, well, I just think you should."

"What's this?" Richard asked, wanting to know all the facts that existed in this secret between his wife and cousin.

"Oh, I was being a witch, and said something about Eliza using her influence with your uncle against me. I know Mr. Darcy was not at all happy with how Will and I were using each other, and he wanted Will to spend more time with Georgiana. Seems Eliza spent time with Georgie when we would escape. I thought she was saying things to... well, it doesn't matter anymore, does it?" Caroline was ready to move off the subject, even if her husband wasn't. She could also tell that it was beginning to weigh on William.

"Oh, before I forget, it seems as if my baby brother is taking after Terrance's example," Caroline changed the conversation.

Richard looked at her and asked, "Why? What did Therrin do?"

❦ ❦ ❦

Elizabeth was tired. She spent all her time either working on her thesis or tutoring. She was a popular tutor, if only because she never asked for money for her services. She couldn't. She held only a student visa, but enough students would gift her with twenty pounds or so an hour that she could get by. As long as her rent remained the same and there were three other flatmates paying every month, she would have enough to finish her education.

But things in the flat were not going well. Mary and her friend, Jennifer, were loud, messy and liked to party. Unfortunately, the parties usually ended up in their living room. Lizzy spent more and more time studying away from home, the neighbors and landlord were beginning to complain, and Sally seemed to be drifting over the to dark side and joining Mary and Jennifer with their gaiety. Lizzy was glad that she would be going home to the States for Jane's wedding; two weeks away would do her good.

Elizabeth looked up to the deep blue of the sky and stretched. She loved coming to Hyde Park to relax. It was a quiet place, even with all the people strolling the paths and children playing in the grass. She smiled, thinking people had been coming to this park for hundreds of years to enjoy the gardens and the beauty. She smiled at a little girl passing by, then gathered up her things and starting walking to the northeast corner of the park. She thought she would stroll past the shops on Oxford Street before heading back to Greenwich.

"Lizzy! Lizzy!"

Elizabeth turned to see Sally running across the lawn toward her.

"I thought I would never find you! This place is so big!" Sally said as she tried to catch her breath.

"Sally! I thought you had a date today?"

"I did, but you're leaving tomorrow, and I needed to talk to you."

"Sure. Do you want to find a nice spot here or..."

"I have a craving for ice cream. There is a vendor there. Let's get one and walk," Sally said with a sad smile, and headed toward the vendor who stood just outside the park.

Lizzy pulled her wallet from the pocket in her backpack and paid for her cold treat, and the two women walked just outside the park toward

Marble Arch. The day was warm, and their treats were melting in the heat of the sun. As they came to a shady spot where they could lean against the wall separating the park from the street, they rested and watched as people made their way in and out of a Tube station while others enjoyed themselves on the patio of a pub.

"Lizzy..." Sally spoke meekly. "I... I think...No! I know... I know I'm..."

Elizabeth listened, but had a strange feeling - a touch of dread and a feeling as if she were being stared at. Both feelings were disconcerting, and she had a hard time concentrating on Sally's slow speech.

"Elizabeth, I'm pregnant."

Lizzy's eyes widened as she looked Sally. "What?"

"I should never have gone to those parties with Mary and Jen. But I felt so out of place..."

Elizabeth couldn't understand what Mary and Jennifer's parties had to do with anything, but she could feel the dread swimming nearby.

"... that is where I met Therrin. He's so handsome, and I just couldn't help but give myself to him."

Well, at least now she knew what the parties had to do with everything.

"I told him today. He... he said it wasn't his - that it had to be someone else's - but he is the only guy I have ever slept with. I can't get rid of my baby, Lizzy, but I'm going to have to tell my parents. My father is going kill me." Sally broke down and began to cry.

"Sally, your father is not going to kill you. Yes, he will be disappointed in you; but he will love you no matter what. I've met him, I know he loves his little girl." Elizabeth put her arm around the girl and tried to comfort her. "He might want to hurt this Therrin guy though."

Sally laughed as she sobbed. "I thought that he was the one, you know?"

"Yeah, I know." Elizabeth smiled at her flatmate.

"You want some company going to Heathrow tomorrow?"

"Sure. You want to come see me off?"

"I do. But right now, I think I would like to do some thinking. I have this strange urge to ride all over the city on the Tube; nothing like traveling underground while you think."

"Do you want me to go with you?" Lizzy asked.

"No. Thank you. I'll see you back at the flat this evening," Sally said as she pushed herself from the wall and took a mad dash across the street to the Underground Station.

Elizabeth watched her until she disappeared into the building across the busy London street. She took in a deep breath and sighed it out as she turned toward the pub and looked directly into the eyes of William Darcy. Startled by the recognition in the man's eyes, Elizabeth fled, taking Sally's path to the Underground.

Chapter 4

E lizabeth was exhausted. The trans-Atlantic flight was long and crowded. She had the "luck" to sit next to a habitual sniffer, and it was just irritating enough to keep her from getting any sleep on the flight. Standing in line for over thirty minutes in customs didn't help her mood, and she still had another flight to make it through before she would be home.

Elizabeth had to smile as she thought of the home she had left behind a year and a half ago to continue her studies. She wondered if it would look the same, smell the same. She had returned to the States only once since starting her postgraduate studies at Greenwich, when she traveled to spend Christmas and New Year's with her mother's brother and his wife. Her own immediate family hadn't celebrated the holidays together last year. Jane was with Charles at his family's home in Connecticut; Lydia and her new husband went to Las Vegas for the honeymoon they didn't get because she was eight months pregnant with the Wickham spawn; Kitty and Mary, who both attended Pepperdine University, spent the season housesitting for some Hollywood bigwig in Malibu; and her parents took a long-awaited cruise to the Caribbean.

The Gardiners' home seemed more like a true family home, but it wasn't hers, and Elizabeth anxiously made her way across the concourse to her next flight and home. She stopped at a Starbucks and ordered a venti mocha with an extra shot. She needed the caffeine to keep her awake until she made it home. She still had a two-hour wait before they began to board her flight.

Elizabeth settled in a seat at the gate, took a deep breath and focused her eyes on the plasma television in the sports bar across the concourse and let her mind go blank. A sound like the whistling wind sounded lightly in her ears, and then gradually grew in volume until it was loud enough to drown out the sound of the people around her. Her vision started to cloud, then opened up as if the plasma screen was just inches in front of her. She could hear herself gasp as the sight of William Darcy smiling at her appeared on the screen. He grinned at her as he had when she saw him in the pub. His smile grew, and he reached out his hand and brushed his fingers across her cheek. "Why did you run?" he asked. She heard her voice mumble words that she couldn't make out. His eyes turned a bit sad and he sighed. Touching her face again, he said, "I will always be your knight, and you shall always be my princess."

Her body jolted her awake as the airline agent announced, "boarding all passengers" to her flight.

❦ ❦ ❦

"Lizzy, I wish I had gone with Charlotte. I've missed you so much," Jane gushed as she hugged her sister in the newly redecorated "guest room."

"I missed you too, Jane. But you had a wedding to plan, and if you had come to London, Mom would have taken over everything." Elizabeth smiled at her sister, only to turn it into a frown as she looked around the room. "Look what she did to my bedroom. I leave, and she stuffs all my belongings into a box in the garage. Then creates this... this Martha-Stewart-meets-Louis-XIV horror. Lydia moved out before I did; why didn't she pack up her room?"

Elizabeth tried to hold back her tears. She so wanted to come home to the sanctuary she had always found in her room. Her studies, her visions, her flatmates and Sally's predicament weighed on her. But now that was gone, and soon Jane would be, too.

"Oh, Lizzy!" Jane put her arms around her sibling. "Don't be hurt. Look at me." Jane wiped the tears off Elizabeth's cheeks. "Mama isn't throwing you away! Don't you understand? Oh, sweetie, she is paying you the ultimate compliment."

"How do you get that from this?" Elizabeth hiccupped and swept her arm out as if she were turning the letters on "Wheel of Fortune."

Jane giggled, "Well, I will say our mother's taste isn't very en vogue, but that isn't what I mean. Lizzy, you have always been strong and independent. You go after your dreams, like getting your PhD and doing it in a foreign country! Mom may not act like it, but she's proud of you, and, to be honest, a little awed by you. She doesn't think you need her. Lydia, on the other hand... Well, I hate to say it, but Lydia will never be self-sufficient. I heard Mom and Aunt Marilyn talking. They don't think George will stay with Lydia very long. Apparently he volunteered for duty in Iraq, and you know what a coward George is. He prefers gunfire to Lydia and the baby."

"Poor Lyddie!"

"Yeah. But you, Lizzy, you are strong, and Mom doesn't worry about you. She knows you are going to be okay. But I suppose she might have told you that she planned on redoing your room." Jane smiled.

"Well, maybe. I guess I don't really blame Mom. This is her house, and I am a little old to be running home to hide in my bedroom..."

"Running home to hide?" Jane looked at Elizabeth quizzically. "And here I thought you came home to be in my wedding!"

"Oh! Jane! I'm sorry. I didn't mean... Oh! Crap!" Lizzy jumped up from the bed she was sitting on and paced about the room a minute before continuing. "Jane, your wedding means the world to me. You mean the world to me. I have been looking forward to this for a long time. I'm just tired. I study all the time. And if I'm not studying, I'm tutoring. Don't get me wrong, I love it, but I am far away, and I get lonely for you, home, everything I know. My new flatmates are noisy partiers. Sally... I told you about her... she told me the day before I left that she's pregnant, and her boyfriend wants nothing to do with her or the baby. That and a few other distractions have me a bit nervous."

"Lizzy, I'm sorry. Oh, I've been caught up with all this wedding planning. See, I should have gone to England with Charlotte!"

Elizabeth laughed and ran to hug her sister. "Well, I'm here now, and I get to dress up and be in my sister's fairytale wedding!"

"Yes, only this time I get to be the princess," Jane said through her laughter. Elizabeth gasped, and her hands flew to her mouth. "What did

I say, Lizzy?"

"Princess. You said... princess."

"Elizabeth Bennet. You have that look on your face. The look that says you're hiding something. I'm getting married tomorrow, and I don't need any secrets clogging up the works. Start talking."

Elizabeth felt backed into a corner. Telling her sister about her unusual visions wasn't what she thought she should be doing on the eve of Jane's wedding.

"C'mon. Tell me. Whatever it is, it's surely going to take away all these bridal jitters I have," Jane settled onto the bed, ready for the long version of the story.

"Well, if it will relieve your jitters..." Elizabeth told Jane all about her visions of William Darcy.

❦ ❦ ❦

Elizabeth smiled as she realized she felt both recharged and jet-lagged. Her trip home rejuvenated her mind, while the flight zapped her energy. She stared at her feet as she rode the Tube from Heathrow. Jane always knew how to make her think, and she had a great deal to think about. She spent twelve hours thinking while on the plane, and now she continued as she listened to the recorded announcement for the next stop.

Elizabeth always believed her mother to be indifferent to her. Jane's explanation of Fanny Bennet's admiration of her second daughter made her view her mother differently during this visit. What Elizabeth saw made her feel guilty for thinking her mother played favorites with her children. No, Fanny loved all her daughters, and was cognizant that each was an individual with her own strengths and talents. Elizabeth's academic and sports abilities were foreign to the very feminine Frances Gardiner Bennet, but that didn't stop her from bragging about her exceptional second-born to all her friends and relatives. Lizzy had never noticed her mother doing such, but she made a point to watch her during this visit and was pleasantly surprised.

The only negative about the visit was that her bedroom was no longer. Her room in the flat was temporary, and Elizabeth never thought to make it the refuge she had done in her childhood room. Finishing her studies and finding a permanent place to live was her priority now. She needed a place to feel comfortable in. The flat definitely wasn't the place, especially with Mary King and her friend Jennifer as flatmates.

The rain was just starting to come down as she switched from the Underground to the DLR, and the pitter-patter of the drops falling reminded Lizzy both of the day of her first vision, and of the rain that fell as she told Jane about her latest dreams. She remembered Jane's eyes widening, and couldn't help but smile as she remembered the blush on her sister's face.

"Jane! You are getting married tomorrow, and you are blushing like you were in a junior high sex education class," Elizabeth teased.

"For goodness sake, Lizzy! That vision was a bit explicit. Not surprising, but explicit."

"What do you mean, 'Not surprising?'"

"Lizzy!" Jane exclaimed and looked at her sister incredulously. "He let you hang around him every summer. When you graduated from high school, he sent you that necklace you always wear. When you graduated from college, he sent you diamond earrings!"

"He gave gifts to you, Mary, Kitty and Lydia too!" Elizabeth reminded her.

"Yes. But we always received a check, and never anything personal!" Jane elaborated. "Hell! You know what he sent Charles and me for a wedding present?"

Elizabeth shook her head back and forth.

"A check for a thousand dollars! I'm not saying that isn't a nice gift, but it isn't very personal."

"But I don't see what that has to do with my dream."

"Lizzy, for someone so smart, you sure can be clueless! He likes you. He always has."

"He likes me as a kid sister not a..." Elizabeth couldn't say, "lover." It was what she had always dreamed of being when she was a teenager. And if she was honest with herself, Will Darcy was what she measured every guy against.

"Elizabeth Bennet, you underestimate yourself!"

Elizabeth stepped off the DLR and made a mad dash for the flat as the rain was now coming down in buckets. As she stepped inside the front door and started for the stairs that led up to the flat, Mr. Donovan, the landlord, stopped her.

"Elizabeth! Welcome back! I've missed you!" He said as he helped her with her luggage.

"I almost had to swim from the train!" Lizzy laughed just as she heard the loud music and banging coming from down the hall.

"Elizabeth, if you can't keep those girls rooming with you under control, I'm going to have to ask you all to leave. It has been worse than ever this past week. I think very highly of you, but I just can't have this. The other tenants are complaining."

"I will do my best, Mr. Donovan. I'm very sorry!"

The man handed her suitcase to her just outside her flat door, gave her a sad smile and returned to his own apartment.

Elizabeth opened the door and looked in horror as she saw at least twenty people inside the garbage dump that used to be her flat. She dropped her bags and uttered a very tired "Welcome home, Lizzy" under her breath.

Chapter 5

Four months after returning from Jane's wedding, Elizabeth was happy that she had claimed the room with the en suite. She awoke early and readied herself for a Saturday away from the flat. She planned to study in Hyde Park, then meet an undergrad at one of the Starbucks on Oxford Street. It was a trek to get to that part of the city, but it was worth it to be far away from the pandemonium at her residence. She gathered all her research materials and her laptop, and put them into her bag. She made sure everything of value was safely stowed away and locked in a footlocker at the end of her bed. Though she kept her room locked, Elizabeth wanted to be sure that her flatmates or their friends couldn't get to those things she held dear.

Elizabeth sighed, thinking it had been almost two years since she had come to England to study. She had planned to only be here for two years, but it was obvious her studies were going to take her longer than originally planned. She seemed to be falling farther and farther behind in her schedule. She almost laughed out loud, thinking she had completed more work on her flights to and from Jane's wedding than she had in the twelve weeks since. She knew she was going to have to do something. Mr. Donovan was extremely unhappy with Mary King and her entourage, and even though he liked her, Elizabeth knew that she was guilty just by living among them.

Elizabeth quietly left her room and stepped over the several people crashed on the living room floor. Ever since Elizabeth returned from the States, Mary King and her friends seemed to spend more and more time partying or clubbing, and every night they would all return to the flat. It seemed as if there were ten people living in the small space instead of the four on the lease. Unfortunately for Lizzy, none of the extra inhabitants paid any rent, though they seemed more than happy to eat all the food.

Sally had moved out before Elizabeth could arrange for a new occupant, and Mary King had quickly replaced the quiet soon-to-be-mother with one of her wilder friends. Elizabeth had managed to dissuade loud and raucous parties, at first, by sending the group out for their festivities, but her influence had waned, and she was even beginning to feel unwelcome in her own apartment.

Elizabeth stepped out into the cool, crisp October morning and looked up to the sky. Happy there wasn't a cloud to be seen, she tugged on her coat, slipped her bag over her shoulder and made her way to the other side of the Thames.

Elizabeth emerged from the Underground at Hyde Park Corner and made a stop at a café for take-away coffee and a bite to eat. It was still quite early by the time she made it onto the path that led along the Serpentine, and she watched runners stepping to the beats that flowed from their iPods. She rambled along, sipping her coffee and breathing in the cool air. By the time she had found a place to light, she had bisected the park and ended up in Kensington Gardens. Finding a place where she could lean against a tree and still be in the sunshine, Elizabeth unloaded her bag and began her studying in earnest.

Eventually, Elizabeth removed her nose from her books and looked at her watch. Not realizing that she had spent over five and a half hours studying, she started at the time. Already close to two in the afternoon, she gathered up books, notes and various scraps of paper and stuffed them in her bag. If she hurried, she would just make her two-thirty meeting with the new student she was tutoring. She hurried across the north end of the park and entered the Underground at Lancaster Gate. She only had to travel few stops on Central Line before making her way aboveground, crossing the street. A few blocks down, she entered the door just under the green circle sported on the coffee store. She ordered a latte, and after receiving her drink, climbed the stairs to the customer lounge.

"Hi, Ronny! I hope I'm not late. I was studying and forgot the time," she smiled at the young man she had met just a few days before.

"No problem. I just got here myself," replied the young man with a New York accent.

"I meant to ask you the other day, why did you decide to transfer to Greenwich? New York has some great schools." Elizabeth deposited her bag and removed her coat before taking a seat in one of the plush "comfy" chairs.

"Oh, well, my mother is English, and my parents recently divorced. My mom decided to move back to the UK, so I thought I would come too."

Elizabeth smiled at the young man, and thought what a wonderful son he must be.

"She lives in Notting Hill and runs a boutique across the way," he pointed out the window. "I was helping her out this morning. That's why I picked here to meet. I hope it wasn't too much out of the way?"

"Oh, not at all. I spent the morning in Kensington Gardens, so it was perfect." Elizabeth smiled and took a sip of her drink. She couldn't help but notice how nice looking Ronny was. She guessed him to be nineteen or twenty and, while she thought he was definitely too young for her, she didn't think there would be any hardship in tutoring such a handsome and nice guy.

The afternoon flew by. Ronny was an eager student and learned quickly. She had a good time visiting with him, and just being with an American again. It was close to dinnertime before the two left the coffee shop, and Elizabeth couldn't resist Ronny's invitation to dinner. It would be preferable by far to going back to the flat. Saturday night usually meant party time for her flatmates, so any chance to stay away was a good one. Dinner led to a trip to the cinema, and by the time the movie was over, it was getting quite late. Lizzy quickly abandoned her new student in hopes of not missing the last train home.

❦ ❦ ❦

The day had started out so well. It was sunny and fairly warm for October. Her new student was handsome, smart and funny, and she even managed to make the last train to Greenwich in plenty of time. But within a block of her flat, she knew her luck had run out.

Loud music blared from the upstairs flat. All the windows were open, and Elizabeth could tell there had to be at least thirty people in the confined space. She could see Mary King flouncing about, dressed only in her knickers, and she managed to miss being hit by a beer bottle flung from inside.

"Time's up," she uttered to herself and ran toward the building in hopes of talking sense into the mob. If she could quiet them, perhaps Mr. Donovan could be persuaded to allow her the rest of the week to find new lodgings. So she ran up the stairs and tried her best to be heard, but it was to no avail. Not five minutes after Elizabeth entered the over-exuberant extravaganza, the police arrived and hauled everyone into police headquarters.

There she sat in a chair with her head down on a desk at three o'clock in the morning. Thankfully, Mr. Donovan had cleared her of any wrongdoing other than her choice of flatmates. Unfortunately, he was not allowing any of them to return to the flat unless it was to gather their things. And so an embarrassed Elizabeth Bennet made a late night phone call to her father's friend and colleague, Mr. James Reynolds of Meryton, Hertfordshire. She put her head on the desk to rest as she waited for the older man to rescue her.

Mary, Jennifer and the latest flatmate, Iris, all had been charged with enough to make them the latest in campus gossip and scandal, not to mention pay a pretty penny in fines. They also sat awaiting their families to come and bail them out of their latest infractions.

Unlike Elizabeth, the trio found copies of Hello and various tabloids with their favorite subject and pin-up, William Darcy, to keep them entertained. Elizabeth couldn't help but be thankful that none of the three knew she had known William Darcy as a child, or about her dream. Pleased with her flatmates' ignorance, Elizabeth sighed and let their giggling whispers lull her into sleep.

Just about to tip over into slumber, Lizzy was pulled from the shades of rest by Mary's loud and startled gasp, while Jennifer and Iris uttered in quiet stereo, "Oh. My. God!" She opened her eyes and stared at the faces of the girls just across the room from her. All three sat in shock with their magazines abandoned on their laps. Elizabeth sat up and studied them for a moment. Just as she was about to ask what they found in the magazine to cause such a reaction, Elizabeth heard a very sexy male voice behind her, "Hello, Princess." Elizabeth turned to see the one person she never thought she would see up close again, William Darcy. The humor in his eye and the soft smile on his face as he looked at her reminded her immediately of another time she saw that same smile, in her dream, just before he told her how she tasted.

Elizabeth couldn't keep the embarrassed blush from rising, and tried to defuse her thoughts by saying, "You weren't supposed to come!" She turned redder. "Er, um... Mmm, Mr. Reynolds was to fetch me. What are you doing here?"

"Nice to see you too, Elizabeth." William Darcy said as he picked up her bag and pulled the chair out for her to stand. "James and Emma are on holiday in the North. They called me." William reached out and fingered the small white-gold suit of armor charm that hung around Elizabeth's neck. "The night 'tis dark, but yours, true. You should but call, and come I will to rescue you."

Elizabeth looked back at the still gawking threesome and, with a small smile, waved. William nodded at the women, "Ladies." He turned back to Elizabeth and said, "Let's go home now, Princess Lizzy. You've tarnished your crown enough for one day."

Elizabeth swatted him on the arm and they left the building.

Chapter 6

E lizabeth kept muttering to herself about being embarrassed as William held the car door open for her. He had to laugh when he sat down in the driver's seat and she was still muttering.

"This isn't funny!" she snapped.

"Oh, Princess, I would say it is," William continued to chuckle as he started his car.

"Would you stop calling me that! I'm not a little kid anymore!"

"I'm well aware of that, Elizabeth," he emphasized her name. "It's so nice to see that you haven't changed. Still fast to get your back up."

"Oooh! Listen, I'm thankful you took the time out of your busy schedule to haul me out of the police station, but I really don't need to be made into a joke! I've had nothing but problems since those girls moved in with me, and I'm sure I'll live through tonight's embarrassment. But besides being behind in my research study, I also have no place to live! It. Is. Not. Funny." Elizabeth pressed herself into the seatback and crossed her arms over her chest.

William sighed, pulled out onto the road, and in a stern voice, said, "I hardly had anything going in the middle of the night, so I can't say my schedule was interrupted. You are not without a place to live, so my saving you from the chain gang was quite funny, especially given the looks on your fellow convicts' faces. Stop being so dramatic. As you said, you're not a little girl anymore."

"Apparently, I'm not the only one who hasn't changed!" Elizabeth huffed. "And for your information, I have changed."

"Oh, I'm sure you have," William said sardonically.

Lizzy turned and looked at him with her mouth open in surprise. When did he become so... so rude? "How the hell you would you know? You haven't seen me in twelve years!"

A red traffic signal caused William to stop at an intersection, and after he did, he turned toward her and said, "We both know that isn't true!"

Though it only lasted a split second, the hurt in his eyes was plain to see. Lizzy turned and looked out the window for a few minutes.

"Where are we going?" she asked with humility.

"Home." His answer was fast and clipped.

"Where..." she couldn't finish the question. The night's strife, the argument and the uncertainty she was facing were about to bring on a flood of tears if she didn't get a handle on it now.

William seemed to realize her struggle, and softly anticipated the question and answered her. "Holland Park. We're going to Holland Park." After a brief silence, he continued, "I spoke to your Mr. Donovan, and he will allow us into the flat tomorrow - before the others - to get your things."

Elizabeth just nodded and tried to ponder her situation. When no answers would come, she shook her head and began to examine the interior of William's car.

"This is a Honda. Why are you driving a Honda?"

"Because I like Hondas?" William said it more as a question because he wasn't sure why she was asking.

"I have the same car. Or I did when I was in the States."

"I always knew you had good taste, Princess."

"But you, in the pictures..."

"What pictures?" William asked as he stole a glance at her.

"In the magazines. Mary, Jennifer and Iris... my flatmates... my former flatmates..."

"The chain gang?"

Elizabeth couldn't help but giggle. "Yes. They liked, well... they... you... um, you just happen to be their beefcake of choice."

He laughed. "Their what?"

"Beefcake, hunk of burnin' love, two dimensional drool candy."

William let out a groan, making Elizabeth laugh.

"Don't worry though, I didn't tell them you were my knight in shining armor. Or should I say, knight in a gleaming Honda CR-V?" She laughed at her own joke. "Anyway, in the pictures they would plaster on the refrigerator or on the loo mirror, you were always getting out of or standing next to a little red classic sports car."

"I suppose I was," he answered quietly, and then after a few silent moments added, "It was my mother's car. And when I go out to those functions she loved to attend, I drive it. It seems to play into the 'playboy' image the press is determined to brand me with."

"Which is why you drive a Honda?"

"Yes! Honda just screams 'playboy,' don't you think?" he said with a wink and pulled the car up to a house. "We're home."

☙ ☙ ☙

Elizabeth awoke and stared at the ceiling. It had been just over a month since her former flatmates managed to cause her uprooting, but now she was glad it had happened, for many reasons. First and foremost, she was back on schedule with her studies, though it had come with a price. Mary King and friends managed to spread the word that it had been because of Elizabeth that they lost their flat. Between Mary, Jennifer and Iris, word spread that Elizabeth was vicious and backstabbing. It was enough for all but two of Lizzy's students to back out of their tutoring arrangement.

She looked around her room and smiled. The room was large, with white walls and an old white wrought iron bed. A rocking chair with a cushion covered in small blue flowers sat off in a corner and a highboy dresser, also white, stood next to a window with draperies that matched the rocker's cushion. A white chenille rug, one she purchased at IKEA, covered a bit of the dark hardwood floor. It was a beautiful room, and Will allowed her to stay rent-free.

A light tap on her door pulled her from her reverie.

"Elizabeth? Are you awake?" Georgiana's soft female voice asked as the door creaked open and the young woman appeared.

"Georgie!" Elizabeth scrambled out of the bed.

"I was wondering if you would like to go shopping with me on

Oxford Street today?"

"Well, I can this morning, but I tutor one of my students this afternoon. However, I'm meeting him at the Starbucks near the Bond Street Tube, so if we don't get lost in the sale racks at Marks & Spencer, I can do both."

Georgiana laughed. "Okay! Um, is this the same guy you were telling me about?"

"Yes. Ronny." Lizzy said with a smile.

"You know, I don't think my brother likes him much."

"Ugh!" Lizzy huffed. "He's never met him. How can he not like him?"

"Well, simple. Ronny is a guy... a guy who will be alone with you, probably sitting very close to you." Georgiana said suggestively.

"He needs to get over it! I can't see how you stand it." Elizabeth said as she pulled a pair of jeans and a T-shirt from the cupboard.

"Well, I always introduce any guys I'm going to be with to him."

"Yeah, and he gives them the if-you-do-anything-to-my-sister speech, scaring the crap out of them! I am not about to let him do that! I'm not his sister, so he doesn't have the right to, anyway." Lizzy said as she padded into the bathroom and started the shower

"I don't think that's the speech he would give him," Georgiana shouted.

"Yeah, right!" Elizabeth shot off from inside the shower.

❦ ❦ ❦

"Morning, Georgiana. Princess. Sleep well?" He said with a smile as the two ladies entered the breakfast room. "You two off somewhere?"

"Shopping," Elizabeth answered as she grabbed his coffee cup and drank half its contents. As she placed it back down, she teasingly asked, "You want to come along?"

"I'm not sure I'd have the strength if you continue to devour my breakfast," he replied snidely.

"Ah, poor baby!" Elizabeth continued to tease him, just catching his smile as he flipped his newspaper up in front of his face.

"Will is absolutely hopeless when it comes to fashion advice, Lizzy. And he grumbles too much. Do we have to take him along?" Georgiana asked.

William flicked his newspaper and mumbled something about only needing three different pair of shoes: trainers, causal shoes and dress shoes.

"See what I mean?" Georgiana laughed. She might only be twenty-two, but she knew her brother felt more for Elizabeth than he tried to show. She also knew that Elizabeth cared for her brother more than she let on. What she couldn't understand was why the two of them couldn't see it.

"I see what you mean. Well, we don't need to drag him along. He'll only slow us up," Lizzy said.

"Mm!" came from behind the paper.

"And we will need to get in a lot of shopping before you meet Ronny this afternoon." Georgiana said purposefully, and watched as the newspaper slowly lowered and William's eyes peered at Elizabeth.

Elizabeth sobered rapidly. "I am his tutor, after all."

"Right!" William snapped and rose, dropping the newspaper on the table. Just before he left the room, he turned and looked at the two women, "I hope the two you remember we have guests tonight, so if you wouldn't mind being home at a decent hour." The last, he addressed to Elizabeth before storming down the hall and out the front door.

"Grump," Lizzy mumbled as she stole his toast from his plate.

❧ ❧ ❧

"Sorry to eat and run, but I must be going," William said as he pushed back from the table. "This is a nice place, Caroline. Thank you for inviting me."

"My wife and I invite you to lunch, and you stop in, sit, eat my chips and then try to run off. What's going on with you?" Richard asked.

"Sorry. I forgot that we had planned to meet." William stole another potato wedge from his cousin's plate. "I'm picking up Elizabeth's parents. They are flying into Heathrow, and if I leave now, I should have plenty of time before they make it out of customs."

"Where's Elizabeth? Isn't she going to go with you?" Caroline asked.

"She's tutoring a student. Besides, it's a surprise... for her birthday," William said with a smile. "She's seemed a bit down with Christmas coming. Since she won't be able to go home this year, I thought I would bring her parents here."

"That's generous of you," Richard said.

"Yes. Well, I'd better run."

"Will?"

"Yes, Caroline?"

"She's still under your skin, isn't she?"

William looked away and took in a deep breath. "Yes, well, it doesn't matter really."

"Why is that, cousin?" Richard asked.

"She has a boyfriend," William said cheerfully, though his eyes let the Fitzwilliams know he felt otherwise.

"A boyfriend?" Richard asked unbelievingly.

"Yes. Ronny Saunderson. He's an American." William clarified.

"Ronny Saunderson? He's a friend of Terrance and Therrin's!" Caroline added.

"Terry and Therrin!" William stared at her.

"Yes. I met this Ronny last week when I went to collect my little brother to drive him north to meet with Sally and her parents."

"Oh, Lord!" William rubbed his brow.

"Apparently, this Ronny and Terry are good friends," Caroline offered. Shuddering, she continued, "I do wish my mother had never married Joseph Younge. The man was slime. Terrance is just as bad. I'm just happy as can be that I don't have any of the Younge blood going through my veins. It's bad enough the monster adopted me and fathered Therrin. I'd keep my eye on this Ronny if I were you, William."

"Right," William said in defeat.

"Will, are you sure he's her boyfriend?" Caroline asked.

"Well, she says that she is 'just his tutor,' but I can read between the lines."

"You might be reading wrong. After all, how many men truly understand the female of the species?" Caroline said with a raised brow.

"She has a point, Will. Don't give up. Lay on a little of that Darcy charm," Richard winked.

"I don't know. She ran away that summer years ago, and she ran away this past summer."

"Sounds like she is running scared, not away," Caroline suggested. "Maybe you need to play knight and slay a dragon."

William was confused, but didn't have time to ask Caroline Fitzwilliam to explain. He needed to get to the airport.

❦ ❦ ❦

"This is a lovely house, William."

"Thank you, Mrs. Bennet."

"Oh, Fanny. Please call me Fanny!"

"Er, I... I don't think..." William stuttered as his sister tried not to giggle.

"Perhaps Will would feel better calling you *FRanny*. Would that be all right with you, dear?"

"Oh, of course, that's just the same!" Thomas Bennet's wife said as she looked at the room's décor.

"I see a distinct difference," William muttered to himself, and Georgiana pinched his arm, letting him know that she heard him.

"I'm sure Elizabeth will be home any minute. She was to tutor a student this afternoon. I'm sure they lost track of time," Georgiana offered.

William rolled his eyes and fidgeted with his wine glass. He looked at his watch and then the door and, finally, back to Elizabeth's father, who just happened to be watching him closely. Instantly William was as nervous as he was when he was seventeen and his father told him that he and Thomas Bennet were aware of the "way" he was watching Elizabeth.

"Georgiana, I was wondering if perhaps you would give my wife a tour of the house?" Mr. Bennet asked.

"Oh! That would be a lovely idea!" Mrs. Bennet gushed.

"Of course!" Georgiana said as she led the other woman from the room.

"Will? Is there a problem?" Thomas Bennet asked, knowing that there was more going on than met the eye. He had a suspicion he knew what it was. Though a dark-haired version, Elizabeth Bennet was the spitting image of her mother at the same age. And if he read the young man in front of him correctly, he would bet everything he owned that the student his Lizzy was tutoring was male.

He knew that Will had been attracted to Elizabeth as a child. Her quick mind and wit challenged the boy, and it was easy to see he enjoyed her company. And he wasn't entirely surprised that the seventeen year-old young man found the newly developed twelve year-old girl fascinating. Though as a parent, it was important that he kept both of them from doing something that neither was ready for.

But now, things were different, and if he wasn't mistaken, William

Darcy, the man, had it bad for his daughter.

"No. No problem," Will answered, still staring at the door as he sipped his wine.

"Will." Mr. Bennet tried to pry the young man's attention from the door. "Will!"

"What?" Will turned and asked in surprise.

"So you think she is interested in this young man?"

"How did you know it was..."

"I'm an old man, Will, not to mention a father. Trust me, you get a clue after a few years."

"I beg your pardon?"

"First of all, if she's tutoring him, he doesn't have what it takes upstairs to keep her interested," Mr. Bennet said as he tapped his temple. "Also, I assume he is an underclassman? That would make him too young, she prefers someone a bit older."

Before William could offer any rebuttal, the front door opened and Elizabeth entered.

"Daddy!" Elizabeth screamed and ran into her father's arms, dropping her bag of books.

"Happy birthday, sweetheart!"

"Lizzy!" Mrs. Bennet shouted.

"Mamma!" Elizabeth turned, and was even more surprised when her mother wrapped her arms about her and hugged tightly.

"Happy birthday, Elizabeth!" Fanny Bennet said with tears in her eyes. She pushed a lock of hair behind Lizzy's ear. "You get more beautiful every day."

For Elizabeth, it was the best present she had ever received.

Chapter 7

With a hug and a wave farewell, Elizabeth watched as her parents made it up to and through the security checkpoint in Heathrow's Terminal Four. She sighed as they disappeared into the passenger area and turned back to William, who stood back, allowing Elizabeth to recover.

"Did you enjoy their visit then?" he asked.

"Yes," Elizabeth answered quietly, keeping her head down in case her tears fell. A handkerchief appeared in front of her, and she took it from William's hand with a sad smile. The man was rescuing her yet again.

William slid his arm around her shoulders and led her to the lifts. "Come on, let's start back."

"I'm sorry about the Tube. My mother was determined to ride it before she left. I just didn't think she would wait until the very last second."

"It's fine, Princess. I don't mind."

"Oh, right! The woman who boarded at South Ealing tried her best to sit on your lap, and I'm sure she had no intention of riding all the way to the airport!" Elizabeth said, still embarrassed that her mother dragged William on public transportation just so she could say she had ridden on the London Underground.

William chuckled and hugged Lizzy closer. "Well then, you will just have to protect me on the way back." He kissed her forehead before allowing her to precede him through the turnstile. "Your father lent me this to help as well." Elizabeth turned and watched as William donned a Dodgers' baseball cap, making sure the bill was in the back. He then pulled out his sunglasses and slipped them on.

"Oh, yeah! That will really help!" Elizabeth couldn't help but smile at how handsome William was. He was dressed in well-worn jeans with a polo shirt, a leather jacket and trainers. The cap worked with the outfit, but did nothing to help disguise his identity.

William just stared down at her and smiled.

"It's going to seem so lonely now. They were only here a week, but I must admit it was fun playing tourist with them. I'm going to be at loose ends today," she said sadly as she stared at her feet.

"Well then, you and I will just have to make a day of it, won't we?" William said as the train stopped at the platform and the doors slid open. "What shall we do?"

🐭 🐭 🐭

Things returned to normal for Elizabeth, and she made great strides with her schoolwork. If she kept at this pace, she would finish in early spring. The possibility gave her a sense of accomplishment, but feelings of sadness as well. The day she spent with William had made her think that there just might be a chance his affections may be a bit more than brotherly.

She sat sipping her latte, and stared out the window, remembering the lunch they'd had after riding the Tube to Covent Garden. Elizabeth smiled, remembering the feel of William's hand holding hers as they walked to Leicester Square, where they shared a coffee and went to the cinema. Lizzy looked into her bag and saw the photo Will used his mobile phone to snap of her with her hands in Colin Firth's handprints, and giggled as she remembered him rolling his eyes over her gushing admiration for the actor.

"What's so funny?" Ronny asked.

"Oh, nothing. I was just thinking about something that happened a week or so ago."

"You want to go to the movies?"

"Oh, thank you, Ronny, but no. It's much too late for a film now," Elizabeth smiled at the young man she thought might be a good match for Georgiana.

"Well, how about a short walk? I need to shake out the cobwebs."

"Sure," Elizabeth said, thinking maybe it would be a good opportunity to ask him some pertinent personal questions. She felt he and Georgie would look good together. She and Ronny headed along Oxford Street, looking in shop windows and talking. After a little over thirty minutes, Elizabeth felt she'd gleaned enough information to present to Georgiana and said, "Well, I'd better get going. I have some early plans tomorrow."

"Can I escort you home?" Ronny asked, standing a little closer to her than normal. Surely, he thought, the questions she had asked had been meant to let him know that she was interested in him.

"Ah, thank you, but no," Elizabeth answered. She hadn't told anyone where she was now living. Frankly, she still couldn't believe it herself. She lied and said, "It's definitely out of the way for you, and it's getting late. I don't think you would make it back before the trains stopped."

"Well... If you're sure. I really don't think it's very safe for you to run around the streets of London alone at night," Ronny teased seriously. "And it is my fault that you have to come so far out of your way."

"I've been doing it a lot longer than you have, so don't worry about it. And it really isn't any trouble," she said as they entered the Oxford Circus Tube station. Elizabeth smiled and waved as Ronny headed for the Central Line. She wasn't quite sure why she felt she needed to keep where she was living a secret from Ronny. Though she didn't think he would tell anyone if she asked him not to, it was better not to put him in that position.

Lizzy headed for the Victoria Line, and boarded the train heading for Brixton by way of Green Park, Victoria and Pimlico. She looked down the platform and noticed that Ronny hadn't taken the Central Line after all, but followed her and boarded the next carriage. Her nerves bristled, and her heart started to beat with a bit of fear. Ronny was following her, but why? Was he just worried about her making it home? He had never done that before. Something wasn't right.

There weren't enough people on the train for her to hide among the masses, so she might not be able to head back up to Bond Street after she changed to the Jubilee Line at Green Park. If there weren't enough people there, she would have to wait until Westminster, pray there would be enough people to camouflage her, and change to the Circle Line and ride it until she could change back to the Central Line and make her way to Holland Park. She liked Ronny, but she didn't like the idea that he was following her.

As luck would have it, a large group of tourists entered her carriage at Green Park, and she was able to slip out onto the platform before the doors closed. She noticed Ronny trying to see through all the heads in the carriage she just exited. She ran for the way out before he could turn and see her on the platform.

Elizabeth managed to make it to the Jubilee platform just as a train headed for Stanmore arrived. She changed lines at Bond Street and headed home. As soon as she appeared from below ground, she knew there was no way that Ronny could have caught up with her, even if he doubled back at the next stop, but she still felt the need to run the rest of the way home. She checked her watch as she made her way up the steps to the front door. Midnight. The last train would have been through by now, but the thought didn't ease her mind. She sighed and thought that she must be missing her parents since they had departed for home, and it was the day before Thanksgiving, an American holiday definitely not celebrated in the United Kingdom. She shook her head and slipped her key in the door.

❦ ❦ ❦

William had grown accustomed to having Elizabeth in his home. Many of the things that he enjoyed about her as a child, he still admired in her as an adult. She was smart, funny and clever; and she was still just as beautiful as she had been as a teenager, even more so. He knew he needed to be careful. No matter what her father said, there was still something that kept her distant. He couldn't figure it out, but whatever that something was, it had made her run that day he saw her just outside the park. He needed to take things slow.

He changed into a pair of pajama bottoms and a T-shirt, and took a book with him into the lounge. He stretched out on the sofa, and planned to read as he waited for Elizabeth to return home from her tutoring session, only the book couldn't hold his interest. His mind kept wandering back to his Princess. He smiled as he remembered the night he found her in the woods, and how the little girl had held his little boy hand and made him feel ten feet tall. He wondered if she would ever be that comfortable with him again. Oh, she was comfortable when Georgiana was with them, but when it was just the two of them, that something always intruded.

He wondered what her student was like. No, he didn't particularly like the idea of her spending time with another male, especially that one, and the sessions didn't usually run this late. He was a bit worried, but she was a grown woman, and if she wasn't home by midnight, he would ring her on her mobile. Her father's guarantee that Elizabeth couldn't possibly be interested in the young student didn't tame his jealousy one iota.

He again attempted to read, but drifted off to sleep instead. A smile curved on his lips as he dreamed of his Princess and their children. During a rather pleasant moment that featured Elizabeth and him kissing, a noise at the front door woke him.

"Elizabeth? Is that you?" he called sleepily.

"Yes," Elizabeth answered as she peered into the living room. "Were you waiting up?"

"Well, I tried. Seems I fell asleep," he smiled and got up from the sofa. "I was beginning to get worried about you."

"Oh, I'm sorry. We had a lot to cover and, well, this week is a special American holiday, and I'm afraid I was commiserating with my fellow countryman."

"Thanksgiving?" William asked quietly as he strode up to Elizabeth.

"Y... yes." She was a bit surprised that William realized the holiday.

"Well, in honor of Thanksgiving, my beautiful Princess, I give thanks that you're home safe." They stared at each other for a moment before William continued, "Goodnight, honey. I'll see you in the morning."

He bent and kissed her lightly on the lips and then headed up the stairs to his room. After he closed the door and flipped off the light, he realized what he had just done and uttered, "Oh, bloody hell!"

Wide-eyed and his head spinning with so many emotions, mostly self-recriminating, he tripped his way into his en suite and stared at himself in the mirror.

"Aren't you a wonder, Darcy?" he chastised. "What the hell did you do that for? You're supposed to be going slow! But no! You fall asleep and dream you're kissing her, so what do you do?"

William closed his eyes and took a few deep breaths before looking at the reflection in front of him again. He could resist one last jibe, "Idiot!"

Elizabeth's hand moved to her mouth, and it was a few minutes before she could manage to move toward the stairs. With a sudden bright smile, she took the stairs two at a time up to her own room.

She took a quick shower, pulled on her pajamas and crawled into bed. Maybe her dream was more than an extenuated fantasy. Perhaps it would happen. She looked around her room. Okay, so may be the bed itself was the fantasy part. After all, she had dragged Charlotte down to the antique store to ogle the damn thing through the window. So what if the room wasn't as big. The thing was, William kissed her. He kissed her. No, it wasn't the romantic woods scene where he pushed her against the tree; but it was a kiss that he initiated and, though it wasn't exactly passionate, it surely wasn't brotherly!

"But he had been asleep..." Elizabeth said out loud. "My luck, he was dreaming I was model-beautiful Caroline, and kissed me with her in mind! Ugh! I'm hopeless." She pulled the pillow over her head to muffle the screech she emitted in glee and confusion.

Giving up on the idea that she could figure out what was going through Will's head, she drifted off to sleep. A whistle alerted her to the precognitive dreams she had become accustomed to having, and soon she stood on one side of a misty window and watched as she saw herself demanding to go home, and then she saw herself standing in the airport handing off a boarding pass and walking down a jetway.

Chapter 8

William tossed and turned all night, thinking that Elizabeth might make his kiss into an excuse to run away again. There was nothing to do for it now, except not to make a big deal out of the happening. If he didn't mention it, and acted as if it were any other morning, perhaps she wouldn't feel uncomfortable. And so he readied himself as he would any other weekday.

Dressed in a business suit, William made his way down to the kitchen to start the coffee maker. "Keep to the routine," he kept reminding himself. "Don't act any different." The two commands repeated over and over in his mind as if they were a mantra that would help him bring upon world peace if he concentrated hard enough. He kept up the mental chant as the coffee dripped into the carafe, and as he poured the java into his cup. He was able to take one sip before his mobile trilled, knocking him back into consciousness.

He heard Georgiana and Elizabeth chattering from the upstairs hallway, and seemed torn between the sounds demanding his attention. The trill of the phone won the battle and he answered it with a brisk, "Darcy."

❦ ❦ ❦

"I'm sure he is nice, Lizzy. But I would still feel better if Will met him first."

"Don't you trust me?" Lizzy asked.

"Yes, I do. It's just, well... You see, not long after my father had his second heart attack and died, there was a guy who... well, he's the stepbrother of my cousin's wife, and I thought he was nice. And I suppose he was, but he cared more about his personal needs than any real relationship with me."

"Well, I understand, Georgie. But you are older now and..."

"No, you don't understand. He made me believe that I was in love with him and we... well, I got pregnant, Elizabeth."

"What?" Lizzy seemed a bit shocked, and stopped dead in her tracks at the top of the stairs.

"I miscarried at sixteen weeks. But as hard as it was on me, it was equally hard on Will. I was only fifteen, Lizzy. He was my guardian. He'd known Terry for a while, and would never have approved of my dating him. Terry's more your age, so that would have made him old enough to know better." Georgiana explained. "I remember Will with such a heart-wrenching expression on his face and saying something about how right father had been. It wasn't easy for him to take the responsibility for a teenage girl."

"What about this Terry? Didn't he..."

"Take responsibility?" Georgie finished the question then answered, "No. He didn't. And he hasn't since. You see, I'm not the only one. Terry hasn't changed much over the years. He has five children by five different women. He doesn't know any of them, nor does he want to."

"Okay. Terry is a creep. You made a mistake seven years ago. I don't see what that has to with Ronny."

"It doesn't have anything to do with Ronny. It has to do with me. If my father were still alive, I would want Ronny to meet him first. I don't have a father now, I have Will. And in many ways, Will is even better than my dad. He's my brother, and easier for me to talk to than my father... about those things anyway."

Elizabeth nodded, and the two women made their way to the kitchen.

"When did this happen?" Will asked into his mobile phone just before taking a sip of coffee from his cup. He turned just in time to see his sister and Lizzy enter the room. Without even trying to protect his coffee cup, he immediately surrendered it to Elizabeth, who finished off the contents and poured more into the mug.

The two women looked at each other and raised their eyebrows.

"Get all the information together. I'll be there as soon as I can!" Will said gruffly.

"Uh oh, something's gone wrong," Georgie whispered to Lizzy.

"I don't care! I want that information on my desk by the time I arrive. Do you understand? ... Good!" Will's voice was even sterner as he barked his orders into the wireless.

"Must be nasty. The vein in his temple is pulsating," Georgie pointed to her brother's head. She waited a moment and then added, "And he's grumpy!"

"Have everything ready. I'll be there as soon as I can. See you then." Will snapped his phone shut. "I am not grumpy!"

"Yes, you are," Elizabeth contradicted and then tried to lighten the mood by adding, "You always are in the morning."

William growled and thought *If you woke up every morning with a raging hard-on, you would be too,* before saying, "Unless the two of you want to ride the Tube during rush hour, I suggest you grab something to take with you in the car. I need to leave now!"

❧ ❧ ❧

Elizabeth climbed into the back seat of William's Honda, allowing the front to Georgiana, and wondered what William thought of the kiss they shared the night before. It was obvious that something at work had taken over his mind. They surely wouldn't have discussed it in front of Georgiana, but she did so want to know what had been going through his mind. Was he interested in her? Or was it just one of those things not meant to happen but did, things that didn't have any meaning? It looked as if she would have to wait until that evening to find out now.

The day passed slowly for Elizabeth, but finally she was headed home to get answers. As she stepped into the foyer, Will was going out, a suitcase in his hand.

"Ah, Lizzy! Good. I'm glad you're home. I'm going to have to be gone for a bit. This problem is bigger than I realized. I'm taking a taxi to the airport, but I left the keys to the cars in the kitchen. Just don't let Georgiana drive Baby."

"If you don't want her to drive your beloved sports car, then don't leave the keys!" Elizabeth said a little too severely.

"Yes, well, you might need it if she takes the CR-V, now won't you?"

He smiled and looked down the hall at his sister, who stood with her hands on her hips.

"You are the meanest brother in the universe!" Georgie yelled.

"Oh, yes, I know, I should be imprisoned for not allowing my lead-footed little sister to speed through the streets in a car that goes with her prettiest party dress," Will grinned with his words, and Georgiana stomped her foot.

"Goodbye, ladies!" William added as the taxi pulled up in front of the house.

"Call when you get there!" Georgiana ran to hug William.

"I promise," he said as he kissed her forehead and then leaned over and kissed Elizabeth's cheek. "Keep that crown polished, Princess." William was down the steps and in the taxi before Elizabeth could think of anything to say in return.

Though he called as promised when he arrived at his destination, William hadn't managed to call again. It had been over week since he left, and Elizabeth gave up on the reasons behind the kiss. She decided that it was just one of those meaningless things, and bringing it up would be just too embarrassing. If it had been more, he would have called her. Chances were that he took the opportunity of being away from home to satisfy things he couldn't with Georgiana and Elizabeth always underfoot. His kissing her was probably the reason he left in the first place. He was getting desperate and slipped by kissing Elizabeth.

"That has to be it! And as for that stupid vision, well, it was just stupid. After all, I have had them where they haven't come true, so!" Lizzy told her reflection as she brushed her hair. She turned away from the mirror and picked up her purse. She looked inside and smiled at the keys to Will's sports car. She decided that she wouldn't drive it, but it was fun just to have the keys in her purse. She turned back to the mirror, stuck her tongue out, then turned and skipped out of her bedroom to join Georgiana for a Saturday of Christmas shopping.

❦ ❦ ❦

Georgiana slumped into a chair and sighed. "My feet are killing me! I'haven't had so much fun shopping in a long time!"

Lizzy smiled at her and set down the coffees they had ordered as she eased herself into a chair. "I couldn't agree more! I spent entirely too much money, but I sure had fun doing it!" The two women giggled.

"So this is where you run off to and do your tutoring, hmm?"

"Yes, well. There is nothing like a Starbucks for studying. Plenty of coffee to keep your brain going, and lots of sweets to go with it!" Lizzy giggled again, then took a sip of her steaming mocha. Her gaiety came to a sudden end when she looked across the lounge and saw a couple being overly intimate in public. She had seen couples making out before, but she was shocked with the two that made up this couple. Ronny Saunderson sat with a scantily clad Mary King on his lap. His mouth was completely covering hers, and it looked as if he were devouring her as he groped her.

"What's wrong?" Georgiana turned and followed Elizabeth's line of vision. "Oh that is just disgusting. Don't people have any manners anymore?"

"It's worse than that?" Lizzy croaked.

"Huh?"

"The guy... the guy... that's Ronny!" Lizzy said before she put her hand up to her mouth as if she were going to be sick. "And the girl is Mary King."

"Your old flatmate? The one who spread the rumors?"

"Yes." Lizzy said, trying to somehow hide by turning her back to them.

"Do you want to leave?" Georgie whispered.

"No. If I stand up now, I might retch." Elizabeth felt guilty for wanting to introduce Georgiana to Ronny. Any guy who would have anything to do with the likes of Mary King was definitely not good enough for Georgiana.

Both women stilled as they heard Mary let out a laugh. Georgiana had a good view of the couple, but Elizabeth continued to keep her back to the duo.

"I wish you would have been able to find out where she lives now. I really want to make her life miserable," Mary said in a voice everyone in the entire store could hear.

"I'm supposed to have another tutoring session on Wednesday. But this time I'll have Terry get into the same carriage with her. It'll be easier if someone she doesn't know is following her."

"Terry might try to hit on her," Mary added.

"Yeah, so?"

"I thought you might have a thing for our poor little Lizzy?"

"That bitch? Fuck no! Let Terry Younge make her one of the thousands in his harem," Ronny spat. "She's probably a virgin. I want an experienced woman!"

"I thought all men wanted a virgin."

"Been there, done that. Now I want experience, babe!"

It had taken all of Georgiana's will not to let out a gasp at the mention of Terry Younge's name. It was Elizabeth's hand that suddenly clutched hers that kept her from it. As if by silent communication, the two women quietly stood, picked up their purchases and made their way out of the coffee shop. Heading toward the Central Line trains, neither spoke until they made it to Holland Park and their street.

"I'm so, so sorry, Georgie!" Elizabeth started, emotion heavy in her voice. "I thought he was... I'm so... I'm such an idiot!"

"No, Elizabeth. You aren't," Georgiana stopped and stared at her friend. "Like my brother says, some people are just very good at disguising themselves."

"But..."

"No! No buts!" Georgiana said with anger. "He was supposed to be your friend, and I realize that finding out he isn't hurts, but better that you know now what he really is. And think of it, you now have the advantage over him. He can't ever hurt you again. Furthermore, he has to put up with Mary King."

Elizabeth stared at the younger woman, and noticed that there was a wisdom she never realized was there before. Georgie was correct. It did hurt to think Ronny had been a friend when he obviously wasn't, but Ronny's betrayal made her understand that Georgiana was more than the young girl she had always known. She was a caring and mature young woman who learned from her mistakes, and decided to be positive about them. More than that, Georgiana Darcy was a true friend, a true and loving friend, who was upset that someone dared to hurt someone close to her.

Elizabeth suddenly smiled and broke into laughter.

"Oh! And that's punishment to fit the crime, isn't it?" she let out between laughs.

Spitting giggles, Elizabeth and Georgiana headed home arm in arm.

Chapter 9

" Georgiana?" Elizabeth interrupted the young woman who sat at the breakfast table with her tea and the newspaper.

"Oh, good morning, Lizzy!" she exclaimed with a smile, putting the broadsheet aside. "Do you want some tea? I made some toast, but I'm afraid I'm not as handy as my brother in the kitchen." Georgiana frowned slightly and continued, "That sounds rather sad, doesn't it?"

Lizzy chuckled, "Well, I don't know about that."

Both women laughed, and Elizabeth moved toward the counter with the coffee maker and began to prepare what normally was already prepared and sampled for her.

"I wanted to apologize to you, Georgie."

"Whatever for?"

"For Ronny," Elizabeth said with shame.

"Lizzy, why in the world do you need to apologize to me for Ronny?"

"I wanted to match the two of you up and..."

"Lizzy..."

"No. Please. I was up most of the night trying to understand why I wanted to get the two of you together, especially after he tried to follow me home and..."

"Wait! He tried to follow you home? What for? When did this happen?"

"The night before your brother left on his business trip. And, as you heard yesterday, he was planning on trying to again."

"With Terry's help. Yes, I remember that. But, Lizzy, why would Ronny or this Mary girl want to cause you trouble?"

"I don't know Ronny's reasons, other than he wants to do whatever Mary wants him to do in order to get into her pants. As for Mary, well, she likes things to be her way, no matter what is considered to be proper, or even kind. I was very demanding about the rent being on time and that sort of thing, which she didn't particularly like, and my study schedule is more my own..."

"Yes, well, you are in an advanced program, of course your study schedule is your own."

"I know that, Georgie. You know that, but it doesn't matter that I had to go through all the undergraduate course study, I am not doing that now and..." Elizabeth sighed. "She is simply jealous of what she thinks I have or can do. Your brother rescuing me from the police station was the icing on the cake, I think."

"Why would she care?"

"She is a fan of the tabloids," Elizabeth said suggestively.

"Oh, gross! She's hot after my brother?" Georgiana grimaced. "I'll give it that my brother is a good looking guy and, okay, so he is rich, but that is just... ew!"

Elizabeth laughed. "I have the same feeling when I think of my parents having sex!"

"EW! Elizabeth! Now I am picturing Will having... oh, that is just gross!"

Elizabeth couldn't help but laugh whole-heartedly. She poured a cup of now freshly brewed coffee and sat down at the table with Georgiana.

"I'm sure my brother has sex, I just don't want to know about it. Ew!"

Elizabeth's humor quickly died at the thought of Will with another woman.

"Lizzy, I'm sorry. I shouldn't have said that!" Georgiana said apologetically.

"Said what?" Lizzy tried to cover her emotion.

"I'm not blind, you know. I know you have feelings for my brother."

"Of course I do. We have been friends forever..."

"Elizabeth?" Georgie's voice was more that of a mother questioning the validity of the statement than that of a younger friend.

"Okay. Okay. Yes, and I think that is one of the reasons why I was pushing toward Ronny."

"I don't understand," Georgiana shook her head at the suggested rationale.

"Oh, I don't either. I thought about it all night long, and all I could think was how angry I was at Will for something that happened years and years ago. I wanted prove in some way that he was... Oh, I don't know. It's all so stupid. I don't understand the logic at all."

"You wanted to prove you're his equal." Georgiana stated matter-of-factly.

"I guess, I don't know. All I know is that ..." Elizabeth lowered her head. "... that I'm not."

"Oh, Lizzy. Yes, you are. You're just different, and that's a good thing." Georgiana reached across the table and held her friend's hand. "I'm so very lucky. I have two wonderful people who love me and look out for me. Will isn't always right, neither are you, but you both help me in ways that no one else can. You helped me come out of my shell after my mother died, and Will kept me from slipping back into one after Terry and the baby. Now, the both of you encourage me to think things through, give me advice when I ask for it and don't push me when I won't. You are always there if I need to talk, and that is worth more to me than anything."

"I think maybe I should be saying that to you." Elizabeth smiled.

Georgiana smiled and said, "To me, you are just as much a part of my family as Will is. You're the sister I've always wanted. And what is family for but to help each other?"

Elizabeth smiled and thought it was a wonderful sentiment coming from Georgiana, but she knew that William felt the same way, and more than anything, she now knew she didn't want Will to think of her as another sister.

❧ ❧ ❧

With the holiday approaching, Elizabeth managed to rearrange her schedule and change her tutoring session with Ronny for early Wednesday. The coffee shop was crowded and noisy with holiday shoppers, and not at all conducive for studying.

It was Elizabeth's plan to make it difficult for anyone to follow her. She would spend just a couple hours with Ronny, to at least show the effort of being some help to his studies, but then would take the rest of the afternoon to shop. If Ronny wanted her followed, she wouldn't make it easy.

"Hey, don't you think it would be better to change venues for studying?" Ronny asked.

"Well, I actually wanted to take care of this now. I'm meeting someone after our session, and we're going holiday shopping," Elizabeth elaborated. Georgiana made her promise to meet her promptly at two in the afternoon. Georgiana hoped that her presence with Elizabeth would deter Terrence Younge from following.

"This is my time, Elizabeth!" Ronny said snidely. Ronny had not offered any compensation for Lizzy's help in over two months, not to mention he managed to persuade Lizzy to purchase a coffee for him most meetings.

"Actually, your time is up," said a deep voice from just behind Lizzy.

Ronny quickly looked up and frowned. "I beg your pardon. This is none of your business." he said as he made to stand up.

"I'm afraid it is. This young lady has a date to go shopping with me." William winked at Elizabeth's surprised and slightly flushed face. "Are you ready to go? I know I'm a bit early, honey, but I didn't think your student would mind."

William placed his hand on Elizabeth's shoulder and bent to kiss her cheek. As he did, he whispered in her ear, "Georgie told me. I've already taken care of this person's friend. Terry Younge will not be following."

"Okay," Elizabeth said loud enough for Ronny to hear. "Let me just put my trash in the bin and I'll be ready." She picked up the empty paper cups and headed for the trash receptacle.

"Mr. Saunderson," William addressed Ronny. "I'm afraid Elizabeth won't be able to be your tutor after the holidays. This is your last session."

"Don't you think that is up to Lizzy?"

"I wouldn't argue with me if I were you, Mr. Saunderson. Your friend, Mr. Younge, can expatiate on that for you if you wish. He and I have... been that route. He's already gone, by the way."

Ronny looked at the older, taller man in front of him, and then glanced to where Terry had made camp in a chair earlier. He was gone. Ronny knew Terry wasn't the type to do what anyone told him to do, unless it was someone with enough power. Obviously the man in front of him had power. Ronny stood stock still and said nothing, just swallowed hard. Elizabeth returned to the men and smiled at William.

"Princess, your friend here says that he won't be needing your services anymore. Isn't that correct, Mr. Saunderson?"

"Yeah. Yeah, Lizzy. Thanks for everything. I'd better get going." Ronny spoke as he took steps away from the couple. By the time he made it to the door, he was running.

"What did you do?" Elizabeth asked, slightly irritated. "Did you threaten him?"

"No." William answered with a smile. "I missed you too, Princess."

Elizabeth stood staring up at him with her hands on her hips. "William Darcy, I am perfectly capable of taking care of myself!"

William's smile grew and he bent closer to Elizabeth. "I don't doubt it, Princess. I just wanted to expedite the matter." He smiled at her as she drew her brows together. "Let's get to that shopping."

"I wasn't really going to go shopping, Will. It was just a diversion."

"Ah, well, I think you might need to."

"And why is that, you big bully?"

William smiled and pulled Elizabeth's arm through his. "I helped you move, if you recall. I've seen the contents of your closet, and you don't had the appropriate frock for the formal Christmas party hosted by Darcy Corp tomorrow night."

"Who says I'm even going?" Lizzy growled, secretly excited about attending something related to William's business. It must mean he wanted her to go as his date.

"I do. I make Georgiana go every year, and since you are part of the life at home, you'll have to suffer it as well."

Lizzy's heart plummeted, but she kept up her teasing. "Next you will tell me I will have to serve the hors d'oeuvres."

"No, but you will have to dance. I believe you owe me one."

"I do?"

"Actually, I think you will have to dance at least three with me. You promised me a dance that last summer. With interest rates as they are, I say three dances is a cheap price to pay."

"You really wanted to dance with me then?" Lizzy gave him a questioning look.

"Yes, Princess," his answer was spoken in a soft, caressing voice. "I did."

"Oh," she uttered.

"Come on. Let's go shopping." Will pulled Elizabeth out onto the pavement, and they began their search of Oxford Street for the perfect dress.

❦ ❦ ❦

Elizabeth looked in the mirror as she put the last few touches on her make-up and thought of the day before. For a man who supposedly had no sense of fashion, he seemed to know all the perfect stores. It was in the second shop they entered that Elizabeth fell in love with the simple but elegant cocktail dress she now wore.

She smiled as she applied a bit of eyeliner and remembered the boyish look on William's face as he presented a pair beautiful black pumps from behind his back in the boutique that specialized in designer shoes. They were the perfect match for her dress.

"I thought you didn't know anything about women's fashions? And here you are finding the perfect accessories as if you knew they where they were," Elizabeth said to him as she took the shoes from his hand.

The sales assistant offered, "Ah, most men have no fashion sense except when it comes to the women they love. Then they just seem to know." Both Elizabeth and William had blushed. And Elizabeth blushed again at the memory.

"Oh, stop wishing for something that isn't there, Elizabeth Bennet," Lizzy said to her reflection. "He loves you like a sister." She slid her diamond studs, which had been William's college graduation gift to her, into her ears and picked up her evening bag.

"You actually look like a girl, Lizzy Bennet!" She winked at herself. With a smile, she turned and made her way down to the foyer, where she could hear brother and sister speaking to one another.

"Make sure you get to bed early," William said.

"Yes, doctor! Will, I woke this morning with a bad cold. When you have a bad cold..." Georgiana paused for a sneeze. "You want to be snug in bed. I just came down for some tea!" Georgie wiped her nose with a tissue and looked at Elizabeth as she descended the stairs.

"Wow! Haaa-chu! You looked fabulous, Lizzy!"

"Thank you, and God bless you! You'd better go get warm. I'd hug you, but..."

"You don't want my cold. Goodnight, you two," Georgie spoke in a nasal voice.

Elizabeth turned to William, and was about to ask if he wanted to leave when she noticed he seemed to be in a trance. "Are you okay, Will?"

He nodded and stepped closer. "You look absolutely gorgeous!"

"Thank you," she answered shyly.

William touched the diamonds in her ears and said, "I have something to go with these."

"What? Oh, no! You've already gone overboard buying me this dress and the shoes and..."

"Quiet, Princess. It's Christmas. Let me play Santa!" He smiled and pulled out a box with a delicate necklace, a fine gold chain holding three diamonds, two smaller on either side of a larger one. He fastened the jewelry about her neck and took her hand. He led her to his classic sports car that sat ready for them just outside the front of the house.

Elizabeth was surprised at the number of people she knew at the party. Many were former and present employees who had attended the summer retreat so many years previous. She visited and reminisced with many, caught up with Mr. and Mrs. Reynolds, ate a wonderful dinner and danced all but three dances with William. In fact, William spent most of the evening at Elizabeth's side, usually with his hand gently on the small of her back or around her waist. He led her into dinner by holding her hand, and when the party dispersed, it was obvious to all employed at Darcy Corp. that the big boss was most decidedly taken.

"You are a very lucky young lady," Mrs. Reynolds whispered to Elizabeth as they said their goodbyes. "You have done what no woman ever has."

Elizabeth laughed. "And what's that?"

"Why you've managed to capture the elusive Will Darcy. Good for you, Elizabeth." Mrs. Reynolds smiled. "Happy Christmas."

Elizabeth frowned as the older woman turned away to slip into her coat. "Happy Christmas." Elizabeth mimicked. She wished it were true. She wanted William to care about her that way, even though the thought was slightly daunting. But though she knew he did care, it was more like a sister. She wouldn't correct the older woman, however. She knew William's actions with her were more of a smoke screen to keep the ne'er-do-wells away. She had seen him do the same with Georgiana at the theatre several weeks earlier when a group of females recognized him in the lobby.

The ride home was a quiet one. The late hour made the trip shorter due to the lack of traffic and, upon entering the house, Lizzy removed the high-heeled shoes from her feet. With a quick, "I think I'll fix myself some tea before I head off to bed," she trotted toward the kitchen.

William watched her slide into the other room on her silk stocking-clad feet and smiled. He whispered, "She's running away," as he hung their coats in the entry closet. He loosened his tie and followed her into the kitchen.

"Lizzy?" he said with a smile as he slowly came up behind her.

She turned quickly and said a startled, "What?" at his closeness.

His smile grew, and he reached out his hand and brushed his fingers across her cheek. "Why did you run?" he asked.

She took in a rapid breath. She had seen this; she remembered this. But what has she said? She couldn't remember, so she just let her feelings flow out, and hoped she didn't begin to cry. "It's time to let the tag-along run off. I know you're kind and allow me to be part of everything. I'm like a stray dog or cat... the princess that you, the knight, rescue. The spare sister when needed."

His eyes turned a bit sad and he sighed. Touching her face again, he said, "I will always be your knight, and you shall always be my princess. But, Lizzy, you aren't a tag-along or someone that I allow to be a part of anything. You are definitely not my sister! I don't want to be your brother, Elizabeth. I want to be your..." he stepped so close that his body was now touching hers and whispered, "your lover."

And with a passion she only thought lived within her heart, William kissed her and continued to kiss her until the teakettle began to whistle.

Chapter 10

William slowly withdrew his lips from Elizabeth's and took in her flushed face. He remembered the whistling kettle just as Elizabeth's eyes started to flutter open.

"You still fancy a cup of tea?" he asked with a rough voice.

"Mmmh?" Lizzy uttered, breathing in his aftershave and clutching his shirt while still holding her shoes.

William bent closer to her ear and kissed the lobe before saying, "Tea?"

"Tea?" she asked back in whispered confusion.

William chuckled, about to remind her of the whistling kettle when the sound suddenly stopped. William looked toward the appliance and Elizabeth, who had seemed oblivious to the noise, suddenly noticed its absence.

"No making out in the kitchen! ... Haaa-chu! .... At least not when I'm around to know about it!" Georgiana spoke as best she could through her congestion. "I'll pour the water for tea, if either of you still want it. Otherwise, take it where I can't see it!" William smiled and pulled the blushing Elizabeth closer to him.

"Hmm, yes, well, I think we'll pass on the tea for now," William answered his sister. He offered a "Goodnight, Georgiana," as he pulled

Elizabeth toward the doorway.

"Oh! Lizzy?" Georgie said quickly. As Elizabeth looked at the younger woman, William's sister smiled broadly, winked, and said, "Ew."

Elizabeth giggled and William let out a "Right!" before ushering Elizabeth toward the stairs.

"Ew?" William raised his eyebrows in question as they stood at the foot of the steps.

With humor in her voice, Elizabeth replied, "Perhaps in her opinion."

"Are you saying that isn't your opinion?"

"Not at all. Mine is quite the opposite, I'm afraid," Elizabeth smiled and put her face to his chest. She drew in a deep breath, letting his scent tantalize her.

"I'm very happy to hear that." He placed a kiss on the top of her head. "In fact..." he quickly bent and lifted her into his arms. "I'd like to discuss the subject a bit more."

Elizabeth let out a squeak and said, "Discuss the subject?"

"Yes. Discuss."

"Oh," Elizabeth's voice turned slightly sad.

William's eyes popped wide open when he realized Elizabeth thought that he meant he wanted to actually speak on the subject. "Princess? Don't you like my way of..." He kissed her slowly and gently then pulled away. "...discussing the matter?" The bright smile on her face answered his question.

"Maybe you would like to drop those shoes?" he looked at the items in her hands. "I think I would prefer if you used your hands to hold me instead."

Elizabeth smiled again and dropped the shoes, noting that they were now upstairs and outside his bedroom door. She slipped her hands over his shoulders and around his neck, then braved her first attempt at pressing her lips to his.

Will moaned into her mouth, nudged his door open then kicked it shut after he managed to maneuver them inside. He made his way over to the bed and gently placed Elizabeth in the center. He crawled over her and continued to kiss her while he pulled his shirt from the waist of his trousers.

With Elizabeth's help, William's shirt found a new home on the floor next to the bed. Will was happy with his place lying next to Elizabeth, holding her, kissing her. He wanted to remove the dress he helped her pick out the day before. He wanted nothing between them, but, more than anything, he didn't want to push her too far before she was ready. She seemed ready, but one thing he had learned from living with his Princess, things weren't always as they seemed, and there was still that feeling of distance.

Though that distance didn't seem so far at the moment.

Elizabeth loved the feel of William's chest as she ran her hands down the strong muscled wall. His hot skin and soft hairs sent an energized warmth up through her hand and arm. She was sure this had to be a dream. Did he really say he wanted to be her lover?

"I think Santa brought me my present early this year," she said between his kisses.

William couldn't help but smile and proceeded to pull the dress's side zipper down. "I will have to say the same," Will agreed in a gravelly whisper. "No. Actually, mine is late. Very, very late."

Lizzy giggled. "What? You wanted me last Christmas? You didn't even know I was in the UK."

"Mmm, oh, I knew. And I wanted you many Christmases ago."

'What?" Elizabeth pushed him back and stared at him as best she could in the very dimly lit interior.

"Let's just say that for a twelve-year-old, you had a very womanly body."

"You dog, you!"

"Woof," William growled into her ear as he eased her dress down her body and sent it to stay with his shirt.

Elizabeth's mind tried to battle with the idea that Will had desired her all those years ago, just as she had him, while her body screamed with the pleasure of his touch. Every part of her that came into contact with him seemed to be on fire. It was as if each particular spot was drunk with him.

She managed to concentrate on what he was doing to her at present, and promised herself to think more later about his mention of wanting her so long ago. Lizzy realized she was completely nude with a completely nude Will settling between her legs. She felt the tip of his erection brush against her womanhood and she screamed out, "Wait!"

In a strangled voice, Will rasped out, "Princess?"

"Protection. We... need pro... tection... I'm not on..."

With a groan, William managed to move away from her, and Elizabeth felt the loss instantly.

"Don't you move. Not one inch!" William stumbled in his darkened room toward the en suite.

Elizabeth followed his shadow, and was blinded when he switched on the bathroom light. By the time her eyes managed to adjust, the light was off again and he was back next to her on the bed and fully protected. It was only moments before William resumed his long-awaited fantasy.

Elizabeth had always felt small and short next to William. As children, their age difference gave William the height advantage, but in adulthood it was genetics. Lizzy took after her grandmother Bennet, and was a healthy five feet, three inches. William, on the other hand, towered over the petite princess standing tall at six feet, four inches. Elizabeth was never intimidated by William's size until she felt him enter her. He was big in every way, and for a moment it scared her.

William felt Elizabeth tremble and heard her slightly frightened gasp. He instantly stopped his movement and allowed her body to accommodate him.

"Relax, Princess. Relax," William said as he managed to keep himself propped up on his elbows. He placed light kisses all over her face and lightly moved his fingertips over her arms. He took her lips with his own and soon she began to take control of the kiss. As her mouth fought with his for control, the rest of her body relaxed and William slipped the rest of the way in.

He moved his hands down to her waist and then placed them under her derrière. He lifted her bottom up and began to move faster and faster. His mouth moved on her lips, breasts and even managed to speak a few enticing words before she finally lost total control and experienced the first orgasm that ever made her scream. It didn't take much longer for William to lose himself, and both fell into an exhausted sleep.

❧ ❧ ❧

A light humming sound brought Elizabeth out of her sleep. She opened her eyes and saw white. It was a white pillowcase and a white linen quilted duvet, she realized, and she let her eyes drift closed again.

They snapped open when she remembered her pillowcase was yellow and her duvet had a flower print.

She looked at the white cloth surrounding her and felt warm and complacent. She attempted to stretch out her legs and felt an ache in muscles that hadn't been used for a long time. Her limbs encountered an obstruction. The obstruction moved, and a hand and arm slid across the skin of her stomach and held on with a strong grip.

Elizabeth looked to the foot of the bed and smiled at the bedpost. Then frowned. She knew that bedpost very well. She had seen it in her dreams, her memory of a certain vision... "Will!"

"Hmmm?" came from behind her and the hold of the arm strengthened, pulling her closer to the warmth radiating on her back.

She looked at the bedpost again, and then around the room. It was definitely the bed and room from her vision, but it was missing a few things and arranged differently. And the wall opposite the window was the wrong color. But it was the room. "Oh my God!" Elizabeth thought. "It's Will's room!"

"You're awfully squirmy this morning, Princess," came William's sleepy voice behind her.

"I... um... need to use the loo," she answered without thought and his arm came away and pointed to the en suite.

"It's over there."

"It's too cold to get up," Elizabeth said speaking the truth and considering that her lack of sleepwear would make it even more so than on a normal morning.

William moved away from her, making her instantly cold, but returned quickly and offered her his discarded shirt. "This might help. My robe is hanging on a hook next to the shower if this isn't enough."

She turned and placed a kiss on his roughened jaw. "You look very rugged this morning," she said slipping her arms into the shirt while still under the covers. "I don't think I have ever seen you before you've shaved."

"I hope I'm not too frightening."

"Not at all. I would have to say you are quite... sexy." Elizabeth wrapped her now covered arms around William's neck.

"I would have to say the same about you. I like the fresh from sleep look... especially on you."

"Not that I got to sleep much," Elizabeth smiled and kissed him again.

"I let you nap after each bout. And if you keep this up, you won't ever make it to the loo, my beautiful Princess."

With another kiss and a giggle, Elizabeth pushed herself from William's arms and made a mad dash for the bathroom.

❧ ❧ ❧

The next few weeks brought more of Elizabeth's possessions into William's bedroom, and many trips to the chemist. Georgiana recovered from her cold, only to pass it on to William and then Elizabeth. William thought he had must have paid enough in cold medicine and condoms to keep the chemist in business for another decade, but he couldn't have been happier.

With Christmas now over and moving well into the New Year, Elizabeth concentrated on finishing her thesis by day and spending time with William during the evenings, nights and weekends. It seemed as if everything was perfect for the both of them. Even Georgiana seemed pleased with their relationship, though she did enjoy teasing them with the occasional, "Ew!" when catching them in an embrace or kiss.

It was a day midweek in March when Elizabeth typed the last page of her thesis and received three letters in the post. One from Sally with a photo of her baby girl in a pretty pink-and-white dress, one from Jane, telling of Lydia's separation from her husband, George, and one from Charlotte, announcing her engagement to the Bennet's cousin, Bill Collins. All the day's news was good, but then again, all of it was slightly disconcerting as well, and Elizabeth couldn't decide how to feel about any of it.

The telephone rang and Lizzy put down her letters to answer it. "Darcy residence."

"Hello, love!"

"Will! What did I do for you to call me in the middle of the day?"

"I'm afraid I have to cancel our dinner plans tonight, Princess."

"Oh," Elizabeth said in a dejected voice. After finishing her thesis and reading her letters, she needed something to look forward to, and dinner had been it. "Do you have to work late?"

"More than late, honey. I'm afraid Richard and I are headed north again."

"Again? But you were just in Newcastle three weeks ago, and two other times after the first of the year! Don't they know what they are doing up there?" Elizabeth said with bite.

"Elizabeth, it's only for a couple of days. I should be back by Friday. It's not as if I'm going to be gone for weeks on end with no way to communicate."

"I'm sorry. I just finished my thesis and..."

"What? Congratulations, sweetheart! Oh, no wonder you wanted me home to celebrate." Elizabeth sighed into the phone and leaned heavily against the wall. "I'm sorry to disappoint you. I know with Georgie off skiing you'll be even lonelier. We'll celebrate on Friday when I'm back. How's that?"

"Sure. Call me when you arrive in Newcastle, or I'll worry," Elizabeth said without any emotion.

"I promise, Princess. I'll see you in a couple days."

"Hmm, yeah. Bye." Elizabeth didn't wait for William to offer any ending salutations before hanging up the phone. She went directly to the closet and pulled out her jacket, grabbed her purse and went out to celebrate alone.

She rode the Tube downtown to see what was on at the cinema. She would lose herself in a film.

After purchasing her ticket and finding her seat, she looked about the theatre and noticed that most of the attendees were couples. The picture was a romantic comedy, and Elizabeth imagined all the men in the auditorium had been either dragged kicking and screaming, or felt that the love scenes might spur their wives or girlfriends into action. She laughed at the thought and turned to tell William her crazy notion and realized she was alone. He was off to Newcastle. And she was off to where?

She suddenly realized that her time in England was very limited, and though she and William had been living together in the same house and same bedroom, there had never been any conversation of where their relationship was heading. In fact, the words, "I love you," had never been uttered by either of them.

Elizabeth knew she loved William. She had for years, and now was positive that it wasn't just a schoolgirl crush turned fantasy. She loved him. But should she tell him? She was positive he cared for her a great deal, but she wasn't sure he wanted to marry her.

As the movie played in front of her, Elizabeth thought of the numerous times William and Richard had traveled to Newcastle since New Year's. Never once did he ask her to join him, even though she knew from Georgiana that Richard had taken his wife with him. By the time the movie ended, Elizabeth had imagined all kinds of scenarios.

She entered the house and felt totally alone. Two and half days alone in this big house with nothing left to do on her research study, no students to tutor, no Georgiana to visit with and no William. It was the first time since she had come to England that she felt she was in the wrong place.

Elizabeth walked into the lounge and sat down on the couch. Staring at the turned off television, she remembered the night before. She and William sat on the same piece of furniture, her reclined with her head on his lap, watching a Jane Austen adaptation on the BBC, and William reading reports and lightly rubbing her shoulder.

"Heaven one night, hell the next!" Elizabeth blurted out. "Well, I suppose I should start thinking about my career."

She rose from her seat and found her laptop. Scanning online notices for positions, she found a job she had always coveted. Without worrying what it meant, Elizabeth applied online for a job as a Post Doctoral Research Assistant at Amherst. Then she had the strange urge to rearrange furniture. By the time William arrived home on Friday, the lounge, guest bedroom and their bedroom had found a new look. Their bedroom also managed to have one wall painted a soft, grayish green.

What irked Elizabeth the most, William hadn't even noticed.

Chapter 11

E lizabeth's nerves were on edge and her fingernails gone. If she didn't receive the date of her oral defense soon, William and Georgiana would go to Greenwich and have a few words with whoever was in charge.

The lack of things to keep Elizabeth occupied didn't help matters. She swore she had visited every museum in London at least twice. More than anything, Elizabeth wished she had a job that could keep her mind off things. Her student visa didn't allow that, and so she was forced into a life of leisure that was about to send her spinning.

The lounge now had a new coat of paint, and one wall in the foyer also sported a new color. Furniture was rearranged in every room, and the attic robbed of treasures to give the living spaces a different look.

Photo albums and boxes now sat piled on a table in William's home office, where Elizabeth commandeered the scanner to digitize Darcy family memories for safekeeping. It was while doing the scanning that Elizabeth came across a photograph that made her want to cry. There, in front of her, was a four-by-six-inch print of the infamous Caroline Younge, wearing a white satin floor-length sheath. Standing next to her with his arm around her and kissing her cheek was a tuxedo-clad William Darcy. On the back of the photo was written, *June 2002 ~ Caroline, the beautiful bride, and William on the big day!*

Elizabeth hadn't really thought about Caroline in years. Sure, she had compared herself to the young woman she had seen that last summer, but she had never wondered what happened to her. She assumed when William and Georgie never mentioned her, Caroline had moved on. Never had she thought that William had married her!

Elizabeth held the photo and stared at it for a long time, wondering if Caroline had died, or if they just divorced. Surely they weren't still married? She could picture them being separated, but surely the subject would have come up. No. They must be divorced, and it must have been a traumatic experience for William.

"That would explain why he's never mentioned it," Elizabeth spoke to the glossy print in her hand. "That would also explain why he's never..."

"Princess?" William called from the entryway.

"In the office!" Elizabeth yelled and quickly placed the photo back where she found it.

William entered the room and smiled. "What are you up to now?"

"Nothing much. Scanning all the photos in these albums so you'll always have them."

He sat his briefcase down and stared at Elizabeth with a smile on his face.

"What?"

"You've redecorated the entire house. Beautifully, I might add, and now you are preserving the family photographic memories. I know you're anxious, honey, but aren't you carrying things a bit far?"

"You noticed? About the house, I mean?" Elizabeth said with emotion.

"Of course. I'm a man, though, and our code of ethics doesn't allow us to admit to certain powers of observation."

"Ha. Ha. Very funny," Elizabeth said and tossed a paper clip at him.

"Stop worrying. Everything will be fine." He moved closer to her and pulled her up from her chair. "You just wait and see!"

"Easy for you to say!" Elizabeth said as she looked at his throat and frowned.

He leaned down and kissed her, making her forget all her worries.

❦ ❦ ❦

Another week passed, and Elizabeth decided that she wouldn't ask Will about Caroline. Why make him feel worse if the break-up had been a nasty one? She did feel hurt that he had never bothered to confide in her, but then again, why should he? After all, she would be going back the States soon, and their relationship would be over.

"I should have realized I was just a convenience; but I wouldn't have traded all this for anything. I may be the dumb fool for loving the guy, but at least I was able to live a bit of my fantasy. I am sorry that my one and only sex vision never came true. Well, at least the sex is glorious," Elizabeth whispered as she stood under the rushing water in the shower.

"What did you say, love?" William said as he searched the bathroom.

"Huh? Oh! Nothing!" Elizabeth said as water ran into her mouth. "I was sort of thinking out loud, I guess."

"Right. Have you seen my cufflinks? The ones with the monogram."

"They're on the dresser," Elizabeth yelled through the wall of water as she rinsed her hair and held her breath until she was sure he was back in the bedroom. When she heard him leave that room, she stepped from the shower and began dressing. She was finally to make her oral defense of her thesis. After being a nervous wreck for weeks, she felt at ease about her research, her thesis and anything they might ask her. What she was nervous about was how she would act when it was time to leave William.

"Elizabeth! You're going to be late!" William said as he paced in the hallway.

"I'm the one who has to defend all her work, and you are the nervous one!" She laughed.

"Yes, well... I just... I just want you to do well. You've worked hard for this. You deserve this degree!"

"Thank you," Elizabeth said quietly.

❦ ❦ ❦

William paced to and fro in the hall outside the examination room where Elizabeth's interview was taking place. He couldn't understand why she was so calm. He was about to burst with nervous energy. She had to make it through this. She just had to! He'd planned everything believing she would walk out of that room with her PhD.

They would go and celebrate at a fancy restaurant, and then go home and celebrate again. The special cocktail party he set up for the next night would allow her to mingle with the best England had to offer. One of them had to be impressed with his little spitfire. They would offer her a position. She would accept it and remain in England. Then after they settled into their new routine, he would take her on a long weekend and fly her to where everything had all started for them. He checked. The retreat was still there. Still operated. They would take a walk in the woods; go to their cave and he would present her with the ring he had been carrying in his pocket for months.

She had to walk out that door with her PhD. She absolutely had to.

William's back was to the door when he heard it creak open. He turned quickly to see his princess with the largest smile he'd ever seen her sport.

"You may call me Doctor Bennet, Mr. Darcy," Elizabeth said with proud happiness.

William didn't bother to say anything. He just moved to her quickly, lifted her and twirled her around before kissing her and making her even dizzier.

❦ ❦ ❦

"Good morning, Doctor Princess," William murmured seductively into her ear the next morning.

"Mmm, good morning, my dashing knight," she said as she kissed him lightly. "Ten-thirty! Goodness it's late! Aren't you going in this morning?"

"No. You know that dress you wore for New Year's?" William asked.

"Yes," Elizabeth answered with a bit of a giggle.

"Wear it tonight?"

"What for? Are we going out?" she asked as she played with the hair on his chest.

"No. We're staying in, but we are having guests."

"Who?"

William just smiled then kissed her and jumped out of bed. Elizabeth followed him and tried to extract the information she desired, but he held her off. When both were dressed, they made their way downstairs for a late breakfast.

As they struggled for who would have control of the shared coffee mug, the front door bell sounded and William let go of the crockery.

"Ah, saved by the bell!" Elizabeth smiled and took a large sip of the brew in the cup.

"Save some for me, Princess!" William smiled and went to see who dared to disturb his domestic bliss.

Elizabeth placed the mug down when she heard a somewhat familiar and happily excited voice coming from the front room. She walked toward the voice and slowed when she heard Will exclaim, "Caroline!"

"Oh, I just couldn't wait to tell you!" Caroline delightedly spoke.

"Tell me what?"

"Oh, I'm so excited! My traveling to Newcastle paid off! We're pregnant!

Elizabeth felt like throwing up. She peered into the room and saw that Caroline was even more beautiful than she had been twelve years previously.

"Are you sure?" William said with just as excited a voice.

"Yes, you silly man!"

"You've just made my day complete, Caroline!" William said and then hugged her close.

At that very moment, Elizabeth's heart shattered and she felt like running and not stopping until her legs no longer remained on her body. But the phone rang just at that moment, and she ran back to the kitchen to answer it.

"Hello?" She tried to keep her voice from wobbling.

"Lizzy? It's Charlotte!"

"Charlotte! Goodness, how are you?"

"I'm great. Lizzy, I called to ask you to be my maid of honor. Will you?"

Elizabeth began to tremble, and a knot formed in her throat. Wedding? Married? William and Caroline. He was meeting her in Newcastle and now she was pregnant. "It's time to go home," she whispered.

"Lizzy?"

"Huh? Oh! Charlotte! Yes. Yes, I'll be... I'll... Yes."

"Oh, good!"

"In fact, I'm heading home. I've finished my degree."

"You got it? You have a PhD now?" Charlotte asked excitedly.

Elizabeth managed to chat for a few minutes and then quickly ran up the stairs without William or Caroline noticing her. She grabbed her laptop and closed herself in the room that she had used before moving into William's.

She logged onto the Internet and found an e-mail from Amherst requesting an interview in a week's time. She replied positively, and then logged onto her travel account and found a flight that would take her back to the U.S. the next morning. After logging off, she packed a bag and left it in the guest room, then slipped out of the house and made her way to the park where she had spent so many hours hiding from flatmates.

❧ ❧ ❧

William stared at his watch and pounded his hand on a table.

"Where is she?" he asked.

"Calm down. You said the phone rang," Georgiana tried to deduce the events of that morning. "It must have been an emergency or something. She wouldn't have just left otherwise."

"Why didn't she say anything?"

"She probably didn't think it would take this long."

"She should have taken her mobile!"

"Will! Calm down. She'll be home soon," Georgie tried to comfort her brother.

William sat, then stood again, not knowing what to do. The guests would be arriving in less than an hour, and the guest of honor couldn't be found. Not that he cared so much about the party; he was worried that something had happened to Elizabeth, and he couldn't do anything about it.

The sound of the front door opening and closing sent the Darcy siblings scrambling in the direction of the portal.

"Lizzy! We've been worried!" Georgiana blurted out.

"My God, Elizabeth! Where have you been?" William growled.

Now that she was home, his worry was turning to anger. "The guests will be arriving soon!"

"Do you need me to help you get ready, Lizzy?" Georgie asked, hoping William would find someplace to relax and cool off.

"I'll help her!" William snarled and grabbed Elizabeth's hand, half dragging her up the staircase. After they reached the bedroom and the door was securely closed, William let loose.

"Bloody hell, Elizabeth! What the fuck were you thinking?" he shouted.

"I just went out for a walk and lost track of time," she answered.

"What?" His eyes seemed to shoot out daggers. "What sort of explanation is that? You lost track of time? Bollocks!"

Elizabeth had never seen him so angry; not as a child and not once since she came to live with him. The sight shocked her enough, she started to tremble with fear.

"The truth, Elizabeth. The truth and now!"

Whatever it was that William might have thought took Elizabeth out of the house, it wasn't anything near what he expected. His shock and surprise showed as she spoke through trembling tears.

"I saw your... your wedding photo... and I heard her... Heard her say... say that she was pregnant with your baby! How could you? How?" Elizabeth began to yell, slowing her tears.

"What? Who? Who am I supposed to have married? Whose baby?" Suddenly it dawned on him. "Caroline?"

"Yes, you idiot!" Lizzy stared at him, not wanting to be alone with him any longer, and began to make her way to the door before he stopped her.

"Caroline is married to Richard! They were married in 2002. I was the best man and I gave the bride away. They have been trying to have a baby for six years! Every time Richard and I went to Newcastle, Caroline went as well. Something about her temperature and the perfect time, blah blah blah! And now, she is finally pregnant with Richard's baby!"

Elizabeth gasped as she stood wide-eyed with her hands over her mouth. She didn't know what to say or do.

William's jaw was still clenched in anger as he stared back at her. Finally he said, "You'd better get ready. Our guests will be here any minute." With that he left the bedroom and slammed the door behind him.

Chapter 12

E lizabeth stood in the shower, hoping the water would energize her, or at least wash away her silly actions of the day before. It seemed possible. At the party, hadn't William acted as if nothing had happened? He held her hand, refilled her glass, introduced her to everyone, stood closely next to her, led her across the room with his hand on the small of her back. She closed her eyes under the spray of water and remembered him kissing her temple and cheek. It was as if the hell of the day and their argument turned into the bright sunshine and happiness of heaven in the blink of an eye.

She hadn't been sure what to expect after the guests left. Georgiana left just before the company's arrival. She was off with friends for a few days in Paris, and Elizabeth would be alone with William. Elizabeth was by no means frightened of William, but she knew he would not be happy when he learned of her trip to the States, and the fact her plane was the first out of London Heathrow the next morning. And happy, he was not. His anger returned, along with such a look of sadness and hurt that made Elizabeth want to curl up and die.

What pained her the most, and what she was now trying to understand, was his acceptance of it all.

"Right, then," he had said. "If you're leaving early in the morning, we should get to sleep. It's already quite late." He proceeded to the en suite, quickly showered and returned to the bedroom in the pajama bottoms he rarely wore. He climbed into bed and turned off his bedside lamp.

Elizabeth managed to wash her face and pull on one of William's T-shirts and a pair of his boxers she'd confiscated months previously. He was already snoring when she climbed into bed, where she lay awake until it was time to get up and get ready to leave for the airport.

Making sure not to wake William, Elizabeth slipped from the bed and tiptoed into the en suite, closed the door and stepped into the shower, where she now stood, not making any headway in her contemplations. Deciding that the water wasn't about to give her the answers, she turned off the tap, stepped out and dried herself. She quickly dressed, picked up and hung her towel, then quietly opened the door into the room with the slumbering William.

"Do you want some coffee before we're off to Heathrow?" A fully dressed William asked, holding out a cup with steam wafting up from the brew.

"You're up!" Elizabeth exclaimed with surprise.

"Of course. Did you think I would make you take the Tube?" His question was voiced in a clipped, business-like manner.

"Um... I didn't expect you to..."

"Of course you didn't. I assume you have a bag already packed?"

"Yes," Elizabeth said meekly. She wanted to cry. He was still angry, obviously. Angry enough that he was going to make sure she arrived at the airport and departed out of his life. "It's in the guest room."

"Ah," he said and placed the coffee cup down on a table. He made a nodding gesture toward the cup and then left, going toward the guest room.

Elizabeth blinked back her tears and watched through the doorway as he found her bag and made his way with it down the stairs. She silently took a couple of steps toward the cup, picked it up reverently and touched every place on it she knew he had. She felt a damp spot along the rim of the mug and knew he had taken a sip from there. She placed her lips on the same spot and took a sip... a kiss goodbye.

The drive to the airport was relatively short. It was a Saturday, early in the morning, and they were out before anyone else had decided to get up, let alone drive on the roads. Will held the door open for her to get in and get out, but there had been no conversation in between. He walked her into the terminal and up to the check-in counter, where he upgraded her ticket to first class, ignoring all of her protests. Carrying her bag to the end of the security queue, he handed it to her, bent and kissed her cheek.

"Try to get some sleep on the plane, Elizabeth," he stated, then pushed her into the roped maze leading to the security check.

She walked to the x-ray machine and placed her bag, shoes and liquids on the conveyor belt and looked back to the beginning of the queue. William stood watching with an expressionless face. She turned and walked through the metal detector, and then collected her belongings on the other side of the x-ray. She looked back out at the queue. William remained there, watching her. She dropped her shoes to the ground and slipped into them and ventured a look at William again. He was still there, but this time he looked upset. He was blinking rapidly, and she saw his mouth move forming the silent words... I love you.

A woman bumped into Elizabeth, causing her to turn toward the intrusion. But in the couple of seconds that Elizabeth's attention had been diverted, William turned away and was heading toward an open lift door. Elizabeth watched as he made it in just before the doors closed.

❦ ❦ ❦

It had been five days since Elizabeth had left England, and no one at work, home or anywhere else, for that matter, would dare approach or talk to William. Any employee who crossed his path earned his wrath. Even Georgiana gave up trying to bring her brother out of his grump, and decided it might be best if she spent time with her friends and colleagues.

Richard and Caroline refused to give up. Both having experienced the pain of heartbreak, they knew it would be best if they could tire him out, so he could at least sleep.

"Richard, you need to take him out and get him talking," Caroline prodded her husband. "It's the only way for him to feel better. He needs to get it out."

"I'm afraid I might have to get him drunk to do that. Even then, I'm not sure he will want to talk about it." Richard shook his head. He had never seen his cousin in such a state. Even the deaths of his parents hadn't sent him down this low.

"Elizabeth Bennet is his favorite subject. There is no way he will be able to keep quiet forever. But the sooner he starts talking, the better he will feel."

"I wish she would just come home. He needs to talk to her!" Richard said with a touch of anger.

"He does. But there was no way he would have forced a conversation about their relationship on her while she was studying or waiting for her oral examination." Caroline said as she eased herself into a chair. "And poor Elizabeth! She has always loved the big oaf. I knew that the first time I saw her. She was fifteen and totally in love with him. It was easy to see, but I don't think she confided it to anyone. I know she hated me with a passion, just because I was there with him."

"I hated him with a passion then too!" Richard growled. "But then again, that was the point, wasn't it?" He smiled and kissed Caroline's cheek as he ran his hand across her abdomen.

"I wanted you to be so jealous that you would come and take me home!" Caroline smiled at Richard and stroked his face with her fingers.

"Is that why you avoid seeing Elizabeth again? Because she disliked you so?"

Caroline looked down and nodded. "She was so young and pretty, smart and vivacious, athletic and brave. Everyone loved her, and she loved everyone. But me. You know I don't handle that well. My parents were never happy with me. I suppose the fact that I was an accident that happened when they were wanting to get divorced might have aided that."

"Yes, well, your father demanding to name you after his favorite mistress wasn't exactly a glowing inducement for your mother." Richard added.

"Yeah, that and my mother wanted to abort me, but my father wouldn't allow it. Then he had to go and die, and mum married into that idiotic Younge family."

"But I always loved you, and I still love you, and I will always love you," said Richard, who was now down on his knees in front of his wife.

"And that is why you are the perfect person to take William out and get him talking!"

'You worked that. I don't know how you did, but you did!" Richard smiled.

"Yes. That's why I'm so perfect for you. You have yet to figure me out all the way. We'll have many, many years where you will never be bored." Caroline smiled and hugged her husband. "Now go and get him talking."

❦ ❦ ❦

Elizabeth's family was slightly surprised to find out she had returned, but didn't question her. She managed to convince them she was quiet because she was tired from the stress of the oral exam and then the flight, but after a couple of days of keeping up a happy front, her reserves were draining rapidly.

Charlotte, knowing Elizabeth, decided to take her out shopping and, perhaps, work out what was bothering her friend. After spending the morning going to various craft stores and card shops, trying to get a handle on early wedding preparations, Charlotte drove Elizabeth to the mall and one of the trendy restaurants that had taken up residence in the indoor garden wing.

"Lizzy?" Charlotte spoke over her menu.

"Hmm," Elizabeth hummed while hiding behind hers.

"What's going on?"

"What are you talking about, Char?"

"You know what I'm talking about."

"No, I don't."

"Elizabeth! What are you doing here?"

"Eating lunch with you, Charlotte. Remember? You asked me out for lunch and shopping."

Charlotte stared at Elizabeth with an all-knowing look until Elizabeth could no longer hold her eye. Charlotte knew that whatever was bothering Elizabeth, she wasn't about to say a word about it. They had been friends too long for Charlotte not to understand that when Elizabeth didn't speak, no amount of coercion would exact any confession.

"Fine. Let's order then. You can advise me about shoes. After we eat, we can go look at them." Charlotte changed the subject. Damned if she wasn't going to at least have a good time. Happy Elizabeth or no.

"Shoes for what?" Elizabeth asked, happy to be onto something else. Something that didn't remind her of William.

"To go with my wedding dress. I have already picked out my dress, but I need shoes. Will you help?"

"Of course," Elizabeth answered with a smile, and the two slipped into their easy conversation of old as they ate.

After eatting, the two traversed the mall and ended up at a boutique of fine shoes.

"I love this shop," Charlotte said. "It's like a candy store of footwear."

"You're telling me!" Elizabeth answered in shocked awe and regard. "This is a woman pirate's buried treasure!"

"Oh, Lizzy! You have to see these over here! I was in last week and saw them, and you came to mind right away."

"Oh my God!" Elizabeth picked up a pair of ballerina-style leather shoes. "The leather is as soft as cotton!"

A saleswoman joined the duo and spoke up, "The leather has been tanned and cured in Italy. The style is popular, and most have been wearing them with floor-length formals. They are very pretty, comfortable and keep your feet from getting too tired... especially if you aren't used to wearing heels."

Elizabeth laughed, "Then they are perfect for me! I hate wearing heels!" She turned them about and looked at the price. They were expensive, but she needed something to help her mood. "I always wanted ballerina slippers when I was a little girl. I used to call them princess shoes because all the picture books used to have drawings of princesses wearing them."

The saleswoman smiled at Elizabeth.

"Then I moved to England and found out the royals wear regular shoes, just like the rest of us." Elizabeth smiled back, pulled out her credit card and said, "I'll get them!"

Charlotte was pleased to see a bright smile on Elizabeth's face, and she forgot about her own task at the shoe store.

As they were waiting for the saleswoman to bag Elizabeth's purchase, Lizzy slipped her wallet back into her purse and stared off to the side of the store. Her fatigue caught up with her and her mind cleared. A whistling sound roared in her ears and everything went dark.

"Miss? Miss?" The sales lady tried to get Elizabeth's attention to hand her the shopping bag.

Charlotte stayed the woman by taking the bag, and then she lightly touched Elizabeth's arm.

Elizabeth spun quickly to face Charlotte, her eyes wide and her face pale.

"I need to go home. Please, Charlotte! I have to go home!" Elizabeth exclaimed. Charlotte nodded and the two quickly crossed the mall.

Charlotte drove as fast as she dared. Whatever Elizabeth had seen, it wasn't a happy vision, and Charlotte wanted to make it to the Bennets to find out what was wrong.

❦ ❦ ❦

After several hours at a pub, Richard managed to get William talking. He let William go on and on until the drink made the slur of William's words too difficult to understand, then Richard piled him into the car and drove him home.

After helping William up the stairs and pulling the shoes from his feet, Richard covered his cousin and placed a bottle of paracetamol and a bottle of water next to the bed. Richard's only hope was that Elizabeth would come home soon. The analgesic would only dull the severity of the hangover, and the same held true of talking. Only Elizabeth Bennet could cure the pain in his cousin's heart.

William lay on his bed and listened as Richard called his wife on his mobile and walked down the hall, then down the stairs and finally out of the house. The alcohol made William feel tired, but his heart hurt with so much loneliness, there was no way he was going to go to sleep. He rolled over and his face met Elizabeth's pillow. It smelled like her hair - sweet and fresh. He pulled the pillow close and hugged it hard. For the first time since he grew past three feet tall, William Darcy bawled like a baby.

Chapter 13

Charlotte willed her car to go faster, only to be thwarted by a traffic light turning red. As they sat at the light, Charlotte drummed her fingers on the steering wheel and turned toward Elizabeth, and worried more as she saw her friend sitting with her hands clutching her purse and shopping bag as if they were lifelines. Elizabeth's constant "I have to go home!" was almost a trance-like utterance, and Charlotte thought perhaps she should just run the light.

The signal changed before Charlotte could put her foot down on the accelerator, and she sighed as she urged the car to speed up again. As the vehicle rolled into the Bennets' driveway, she watched as Elizabeth flew from the car before it had come to a complete stop and ran into the house, still clutching her bags. Charlotte followed after turning off the engine. What she found when she entered the house only confused her.

Elizabeth stood in the middle of the kitchen, her whole body shaking, and Mr. and Mrs. Bennet and Lydia staring at her as if she had lost her mind.

"Gee, Charlotte! What did you do to Lizzy?" Lydia snorted.

"She had a vi..., er she said she had to come home." Charlotte shrugged.

Elizabeth nodded and said through her tears, "Daddy, please! I have to go home!"

"You are home, stupid!" Lydia clucked.

"Lydia!" Mrs. Bennet scolded her youngest, then turned to Elizabeth. In her softest motherly voice said, "What happened, Lizzy?"

"I... I... s-saw h-him! H-he... H-he..." Elizabeth couldn't go on and broke into sobs as she wrapped her arms around her middle, her bags slapping against her body.

"Charlotte, what happened? Who did she see?" Mr. Bennet inquired.

"Um, well..." Charlotte struggled with what to say. It was one thing to tell complete strangers in a pub that Elizabeth "saw" things, but her parents? When still very young, Elizabeth had made Charlotte promise never to tell anyone about the psychic dreams. And though Charlotte let the "secret" slip from her lips on occasion, it could always be explained as a goofy story to liven up a party or group. No one really paid much attention to the validity of it.

"Charlotte, please!" Mr. Bennet implored her.

She looked over at Elizabeth and then each person in the room. She returned her eyes back to Elizabeth and said, "I don't know whom she saw, but she zoned out and saw something. When she came out of it, she was pale and demanded to come home. I thought she meant here."

"Zoned out? Ha! What a joke! Lizzy's been zoned out her whole life!" Lydia snickered.

"Lydia! Shush! This doesn't concern you! Lizzy is having a hard enough time of it," Mrs. Bennet said to her youngest.

"Lizzy? Hard time? That's a laugh! I have a wayward husband who is demanding a divorce, and a crying, eighteen month-old brat. I don't see how she has it hard."

"Lydia!" Mrs. Bennet cried with her hand pointing at her mouthy daughter. "You purposefully got yourself pregnant, thinking being a military wife was 'so cool,' and as for your daughter... she spends more time with your father and me than she does with you! Thank goodness you've had your tubes tied!"

"H-how did you know that?" Lydia interjected, but it seemed to have no effect on Mrs. Bennet's tirade.

"Lizzy will be a much more loving parent to her five children than you are to Sunni Delight!"

"Huh?" Lydia said as Mr. Bennet whispered to his wife, "I thought you said six?"

"I told you, Tom! It's a surprise!" Mrs. Bennet shook her head at her husband.

"Oh, yes. That's right," Tom Bennet nodded. "Fanny, maybe you should take Lizzy upstairs. Charlotte, would you like a soda pop, or maybe some tea?"

"Daddy! Please!" Elizabeth said imploringly. "I have to go home!"

Tom Bennet went to his daughter, kissed her forehead and said, "You shall, sweetie. You go on up with your mother, and I'll get Charlotte something and then make some calls. All right?"

Elizabeth didn't have time to answer as her mother led her from the kitchen and upstairs to the master bedroom.

❧ ❧ ❧

Fanny Bennet guided her daughter to the window seat that faced the expansive backyard and sat down, pulled the bags from her daughter's hands, then pulled Elizabeth down to sit with her.

"Tell me about your vision, Lizzy," Fanny instructed her daughter.

Elizabeth stared at her mother with her mouth slightly agape.

"Oh come, come, Elizabeth. I'm your mother. Did you think that I didn't know?" Fanny smiled, wiping her daughter's face with a tissue she pulled from a box on the nearby table.

Elizabeth looked at her mother's face, and saw the loving eyes and sweet smile she remembered her mother always had for her when she was small, and which comforted her after falling and skinning her knee or elbow.

"Do you think you just were graced with this ability?" Elizabeth just stared at her. "Here, lie down and put your head on my lap."

Elizabeth did as she was told, and stared out the window at the tree she loved to climb in her younger years, and started to relax as her mother stroked her hair.

"Your Grandma Gardiner had them, you know?" Mrs. Bennet mentioned.

"She did?"

"Yes, Lizzy. And so do I."

Elizabeth turned and looked up at her mother in surprise.

"Why do you think I changed your room and not Lydia's?"

"I thought..." Elizabeth was about to say that Lydia was her favorite, but she wasn't so sure anymore.

"I knew you would find a home with Will, and I knew Lydia would be back; though I think we will be keeping Sunni, and Lydia will be off somewhere 'cool.'"

Elizabeth sat up a bit, and Mrs. Bennet hugged her to her chest.

"Now tell me what you saw, Lizzy. Whatever it is, I can see it is making you hurt. Is it William?"

"Y-yes. H-he... H-he..." Elizabeth started to sob again.

"Let me see if I can help you," Fanny said keeping her daughter close. "I would have to say that this vision did not include you in it but it did William. Am I correct so far?"

Elizabeth nodded.

"Did you and William have a disagreement?"

Elizabeth nodded again.

"I'm afraid I don't know what you saw, Lizzy, but from how I see you feel, I can only imagine that William is feeling some sort of pain. And from the look of your reaction, I can only assume it is emotional pain."

Elizabeth looked up at her mother and nodded.

"I understand. It's hard to 'vision' that. We understand our own emotional pain. We know where it will hurt, and when things happen, we know where we will feel it. It hurts, and we've learned over the years to deal with it. But when we vision someone we love and feel their pain, it isn't the same as our own. Everyone's pain is felt in a unique place. You felt William's, and the pain is excruciating. I assume even more so since it concerns his feelings for you?"

"I'm such an idiot. I didn't think he felt the same way about me as I do him. I thought I was just someone convenient. We argued and then at the party he acted as if nothing had happened and..." Elizabeth sat up straight and her hand flew to her mouth. "The party! Oh, my God!"

"What, Lizzy?" Mrs. Bennet asked in a soothing voice.

"The party was for... me! He threw the party for me! All the guests were..." Elizabeth started to cry again. "I'm such an idiot!"

Mrs. Bennet chuckled lightly. "No. Lizzy, you're not. You've had a lot to deal with. Even if you are gifted with some special views into the future, it doesn't mean you aren't a normal person."

"Some visions! They don't always come true, so I don't trust them."

"Oh, my! They always come true, Lizzy. Some way or another, they all do. Have you been doubting them?"

Elizabeth didn't answer, but Mrs. Bennet didn't need her to.

"Lizzy, why do you doubt them?"

"The first one I remember... when I was in the cave at the lake when I was five... I dreamt that I would be rescued by a knight. My knight looked just like Will and, of course, Will found me. But in the dream, when he led me back, Jane stomped her foot and I had this very pretty princess dress on. I didn't have on a princess dress, I was in muddy shorts and a T-shirt and had a dirty face. Jane hugged me, she didn't stomp her foot!"

Mrs. Bennet smiled. "Is this the only vision that has been... inaccurate?"

"Well, no. There have been others, but not many. And come to think of it, most of them did eventually work out, but the first one and one other... no."

"Elizabeth, hear me. Do. Not. Doubt. Them. You will understand one day, and I am sure it will be soon. But let us go back to your latest vision. Do you doubt it?"

"No. It hurt too much not to be real." Elizabeth hugged her mother tightly. "He was crying, Mom." Elizabeth spoke tearfully. "He was on my side of the bed, hugging my pillow and crying."

"Your side of the bed, hmm?" Fanny smiled as Elizabeth stiffened. "Oh, pooh, Elizabeth! I wasn't born yesterday. I know you two kept separate rooms while your father and I visited, but I told him that would soon change and this time he couldn't do anything about it."

"This time?"

"Yes. You must have William tell you about it." Mrs. Bennet smiled and tucked Elizabeth's hair behind her ears. "Now let's go down and see how well your father has done about getting you home."

❦ ❦ ❦

Tom Bennet managed to get Elizabeth on the first morning flight the following day, and Elizabeth didn't complain when her father sent her back to England in the first class cabin. She felt sorry for the passengers in coach. They didn't know what they were missing. Even if she didn't sleep, lying down and resting for most of the flight was much better than sitting the whole way. She just wished the plane would fly faster. She wanted to get home to William and tell him that she loved him and was sorry for being such a dolt.

Elizabeth smiled into her pillow as she thought of William and how much he must love her. He let her redecorate the house, for goodness sake! And she never even asked. "That's gotta be love!" Elizabeth whispered.

Elizabeth's eyelids fluttered closed, and she hoped that her mother was able to get through to Georgiana and ask her to pick her up at the airport. Elizabeth felt bad about calling Amherst and leaving a message on the human resources voicemail. She wondered if they called back, and what her mother would tell them. She couldn't help but giggle out loud imagining her mother's voice in her head. "I'm so sorry. My daughter won't be able to make the appointment. She needed to get back to England and soothe her boyfriend... if you know what I mean."

Elizabeth buried her face in the pillow, slightly embarrassed to remember how she and her mother packed her suitcase and talked about sex, of all things. Did she really tell her mother that William could make putting on a condom sexy? God, she even told her that their condom ritual had become a game of sorts! Her mother didn't seem shocked, however. But Elizabeth was shocked when her mother hugged her goodbye and whispered in her ear, "Forget the condoms, dear. Just make me some beautiful grandbabies."

Chapter 14

Elizabeth stood in the airport, looking about for Georgiana. It was possible that her mother couldn't get in touch with her, or that she might be checking the airline desk to see about flight status. Elizabeth decided to wait a bit longer, and then, if necessary, take a taxi to Holland Park. She would take the Tube, but the hour was late, and since Ronny had followed her, Elizabeth had tended to stay away from the Underground at night.

"Elizabeth!" She turned toward the unexpected voice.

"C-Caroline?" Elizabeth asked surprised.

"Yes, sorry. Your Mum phoned and Georgiana was out, so I told her I would come to pick you up." Caroline explained as she took Elizabeth's hand and pulled her toward the car park. "I haven't said a word to William, though Richard and I are so happy you're home. Will has been an absolute tyrant without you."

"Oh, um..." Elizabeth didn't know what to say to Caroline. She hadn't been prepared to see the woman.

Caroline stopped suddenly, lowered her head and spoke quietly, "I want to apologize to you. You've been with William for months now, and I've been determined to stay away. I remember that summer in the States, and how much you disliked me, and I was so jealous of you..."

"Of me? Whatever for? I was jealous of you!"

"You have everything, Elizabeth. A loving family, a guy who was head over heels for you, you were pretty... and even more so now. You're smart and fun. And have curves to die for!" Caroline explained. "And why on Earth would you be jealous of me?"

Elizabeth thought back to the day she sat in the tree and decided to hate Caroline Younge for the rest of her life, and suddenly felt totally ashamed for it. "You looked like a model; tall, with all the latest fashions fitting you perfectly. I thought you were the most beautiful girl I'd ever seen, even more so than my sister, Jane. And you were with Will." Elizabeth thought it was best to come clean. She had never told anyone about sitting in that tree, but right then and there, she knew it was time to let the past go. "I was sitting up in a tree looking over the lake when you and Will suddenly appeared below. He... he... he kissed you, and was trying to get you to... um... do it in the woods. I decided to hate you forever right then and there. I wanted to be the one he... well, you get the picture."

Caroline stood there with one hand covering her open mouth and the other still holding Elizabeth's hand. After a moment, she began to pull Elizabeth toward the car park again. "Let me tell you something as I drive you home."

As Caroline navigated the roads, she explained the whole relationship she'd had with William that summer.

"So you see, we never did anything, nor were we likely to. It was a game to make us feel better. I wanted Richard and William wanted you. Sure, I let him kiss me. I needed the affirmation just as much as he did. I think if we ever had weakened and done the deed, we would have regretted it. And we knew that. But William had already been lectured by his father when your father requested it."

"My father requested it?" Elizabeth asked when they stopped at a traffic light.

"Yes, he was seventeen, and apparently had a hard time not looking at you. The lecture had embarrassed him so much that he refused to attend the retreats after that. It was only when his mother died that he... Anyway, he knew his feelings hadn't changed, and when he saw you again, well... You were fifteen, and he was still too old for you."

Caroline reached over to her passenger. "Elizabeth, William Darcy has been in love with you since he was a boy. Only when he was older, did he realize it. He has never gone out with the same woman more three times and you, he moves in and lets redecorate the place without a word. That has to tell you something."

Elizabeth nodded. "Yes. It does now. I... I have been hiding within myself for so long that I've stopped looking at everything around me."

Caroline pulled up in front of the Darcy townhouse and turned to look at Elizabeth. "You know, I understand that. And sometimes we have to do that for our own sanity, but it's like wearing sunglasses. You need to take them off when it gets dark, or you will never see what's right in front of you."

Elizabeth laughed and then leaned over and hugged the one person she never thought she would want to call a friend. "One thing I don't understand is why William or Georgie never mentioned that you were Richard's wife."

"You didn't know Richard was married?" Caroline asked with a look of shock on her face.

"Oh, I knew he was married! They just always called you 'Richard's wife' and never Caroline."

Caroline laughed and then shook her head. "I'm afraid that is my fault. I'll have to tell you sometime, but right now, I think you'd better go take care of that big oaf in there."

Elizabeth nodded happily and jumped out of the car, grabbed her luggage and took the front steps two at a time.

❧ ❧ ❧

The house was dark. She looked at her watch. It was late, and Elizabeth knew that everyone would have to be in bed. She took a deep breath, dropped her luggage and ascended the staircase, letting her fingers trace the handrail as she went.

At the top, Elizabeth looked down the hall and looked along the floor, checking for light seeping out from thresholds. All dark. She continued to the master suite with a smile on her face. She opened the door quietly and entered softly. Light shone in from the window, and she could see William sleeping in the middle of the bed with her pillow held tightly in his clutches. His face, though peaceful, showed traces of sadness. She kept her eye on him as she toed off her shoes and crept nearer.

She stood watching him sleep. Her heart felt full, and she wanted nothing more than to have him hold her as he was holding the pillow.

She stripped out of her clothes and climbed on the bed clad only in her bra and panties.

William stirred but remained asleep, though she was sure he had called her name. She leaned down and lightly kissed his lips, holding them on his until she knew he was awake.

"Hi," she said softly.

"Lizzy?" William asked sleepily. "Am I dreaming?"

"No. I'm home," she said as she lay her head down on his bare chest. "I'm so sorry, Will! I should have never left. I..." Tears began to fall from her eyes. "I love you."

"Oh, Princess!" Will exclaimed softly as he pulled her up and brushed her tears from her cheeks. "Don't cry, my sweet, beautiful love. I love you too, you silly woman."

Will pulled her down so her lips met his and kissed her as if his life depended on it. He pushed off the covers and managed to rid Elizabeth of her undergarments, then made sure his boxers joined the other clothes on the floor.

Keeping his lips on hers, he arranged her to sit astride him then buried his hands in her hair.

In a gruff voice, he growled, "Don't you ever run away again, do you hear me?"

"Never, ever again!" she answered him and watched as he fell back on the pillow.

"I thought I was going to have to live the rest of my life without you, Elizabeth! I don't think that's possible." And skipping any foreplay or their customary condom ritual he lifted her and placed her above his already straining erection.

Elizabeth lowered herself onto him with a deep sigh as she tilted her head back. She opened her eyes and looked at the ceiling, all at once realizing she was in her room, on her bed, with her man deep inside her filling her full and tight. Everything felt so wonderful. She smiled as she felt her breasts tingle and looked down at them.

William was now sitting up and pinching her right nipple with his fingers and sucking on her left.

"God, you taste so good, Princess." Will groaned and slipped his hands down to her legs and held on so that he could lift her and arrange her so she was lying down. He stopped short and kept her upright and he sat up on his knees and began to move her up and down.

Elizabeth gripped his arms tightly and felt the pressure build rapidly and within just a few moments traveled with her climax as if she were surfing on lava as a volcano erupted. She didn't quite understand how she made it to a full reclining position, but she was now on her back, and Will began to frantically move in and out of her. She wrapped her legs around him and held fast. As he came, Will pulled her into his arms and held her tightly.

Elizabeth knew at that moment she was in her true home. Her mother was right, the visions all seemed to come true. Well, all of them but the princess dress. But at that moment, she didn't give a hoot about any princess dress.

The couple held each other tightly, and William pulled the covers over them.

"Will?"

"Hmm?"

"I'm sorry I doubted you, us, everything. I..."

"Shh, Princess," William said as he pressed his finger to her lips. "We'll talk about it in the morning. Sleep. You're exhausted."

Elizabeth looked at him and tried to speak again. William quickly covered her lips with his.

When he broke the kiss, he said, "We have a lot to discuss, but right now, the only communication we need is just simple loving." He turned and looked at the clock. He turned back to her and continued, "Tomorrow you can tell me why you were obviously sitting on airplane when you were supposed to be in an interview."

Elizabeth watched his eyes and opened her mouth to answer him.

He stopped her by saying, "Tomorrow," and pulled her closer to him.

When she heard his breathing begin to slow into sleep, she whispered, "Because I belong home with the man I love. I belong with you."

He squeezed her gently and pressed his lips into her hair.

After a few more minutes, they were both fast asleep, held tightly in each other's arms.

Chapter 15

Elizabeth awoke to sunlight shining through the windows - her bedroom windows. She smiled, remembering William's welcome last night. Her smile broadened as she again realized her homecoming was her vision in the pub when Charlotte was visiting. She turned so she could cuddle up to his warm body.

But William wasn't there.

Elizabeth sat up, worried it had all been a dream, or that he really hadn't wanted her to come back. He'd said they would talk.

"Talk?" she uttered aloud. "Maybe he wasn't saying, 'Welcome home.' Maybe it was 'Goodbye.'"

Confused and terrified, Elizabeth found herself frozen on the bed as she held the sheet up to cover her breasts and felt the tears slip from her eyes. She tried with all her might to keep the sobs from escaping and she closed her eyes in hope of finding help from the darkness.

"Lizzy! What's wrong?" William hurried to the bed, setting down a tray on a nearby table.

Elizabeth opened her eyes as he wrapped his arms about her. "Why are you crying?"

"I woke up and you were gone... I... I th-thought... thought that y-you..."

"Shh. Elizabeth. No. I'm not gone. I'm not going anywhere." William wiped the tears from her cheeks. "And neither are you. We agreed to that last night, remember?"

Elizabeth nodded. She instantly felt as if she was five years old again, and William was saving her from the frightening shadows of the cave.

"Let me close the door," William said as he rose from the bed and headed for the room's open portal.

Elizabeth followed him with her eyes, and noticed that her luggage had been brought up and placed by the closet door. "You brought up my bag?"

"Yes, love. I didn't think you wanted it as a permanent fixture in the foyer." He winked, and Elizabeth smiled. William returned to the bed and removed his robe and slid back under the sheets. He reached over and picked up a large mug of coffee and took a sip.

"It's still a bit warm, but drinkable," he said as he handed the mug to Elizabeth. "I thought we could share as we talked."

Elizabeth sipped and waited for William to begin.

"Why did you run away, Lizzy? I don't understand. I've never understood. The first time was that last summer. You weren't ill, were you?"

"No," Elizabeth looked at the coffee in the cup, took a sip and began her story of a little girl who had fallen for a young boy, only for that boy to grow into a man while she seemed to remain a child.

She felt she must have rambled on and on, not sure of what her point was, but William seemed to understand all of what she was saying. Suddenly tears began to trickle from her eyes as she remembered turning twelve and developing, and feeling horribly ugly.

"Everyone would stare at me. I was so embarrassed all the time. I ended up with all of Jane's hand-me-downs, and they didn't quite fit. And you stopped talking to me."

William chuckled. "I'm sorry, Princess! That little blue bikini got me into a world of trouble!"

"What?"

"I was one of those who stared, love," William said as he watched Elizabeth's stunned and hurt expression. "You were the most beautiful female I had ever seen. You had the body of a twenty year-old woman.

I couldn't help looking."

"I did not! I ..."

"Elizabeth! You were gorgeous, and even more so now. Your body matured young and quickly. I can understand that it was difficult to understand everything at that time, but you surely can see it now."

"Yes, I can see that part of it, but... but w-why did you stop talking to me?"

William wiped his hand over his face and signed. He took the cup and sipped the now cold coffee, grimaced, closed his eyes and explained.

"I would stare at you. I was fascinated by all your curves. You were still my Princess, but yet you had changed into a hypnotic siren that called to my hormones. I would go to the cave and... Oh, Lord. Well, let's just say that I took care of anything that would cause me to be embarrassed."

Elizabeth started to laugh. "Are you saying I got you all hot and bothered?"

"Extremely!"

"But why wouldn't you talk to me? I mean, I would think that..."

"Lizzy! I couldn't talk to you. If I got too close to you, I would have scared you to death! Besides, your father had my father take me aside and, well." William stopped and turned away from Elizabeth.

"What?"

"Apparently, your father had witnessed one of my excursions to the cave."

"He saw you whacking your willie?" Elizabeth chuckled and William gave her the evil eye.

"Yes. He also heard me."

"Heard you?"

"I was fantasizing about you while I... well, I called out your name." William's face turned beet red at the memory, and Elizabeth hugged him tightly, and soon the talking stopped and a repeat performance of the night before evolved.

After a shower and lunch, William and Elizabeth made their way out of the house and walked to and all over Hyde Park. By the time the sun started to set, they had cleared the air of many things.

❧ ❧ ❧

"Okay, explain something to me," Elizabeth requested as she and William sat down to dinner. "Why is it that neither you nor Georgiana refer to Caroline by name. You always say, 'Richard's wife.' You call her Caroline to her face, right?"

William smiled and picked up his wine glass. After taking a sip, he replied, "Caroline has had a hard time of it. Her parents were in the midst of a divorce when her mother realized she was pregnant. Neither Catherine, her mother, nor Lewis, her father, wanted to have her born into a broken home, so they decided to stay married.

"Catherine wanted to name her Anne, but Lewis insisted on Caroline, so she became Caroline Anne de Bourgh. It wasn't until she was about three or four months old that Catherine discovered why Lewis wanted to name her so. He was having an affair with a woman by the name of Carol Lynne Miller."

"Oh my! Are you serious?"

"Quite! Well, Catherine insisted on calling her Anne after that. Poor girl was confused with one parent calling her one name and the other another. Then her father died, and it wasn't all that long before her mother remarried a man by the name of Younge. He seemed to think it was funny that her father named her after his mistress, and made fun of her quite a bit. He adopted her, but never really cared for her. Caroline used to tell everyone her name was Sally Smith.

"Then she met Richard. He didn't care about her name, he only loved her. Not counting the summer she came to the States, they were together constantly."

"She told me about that summer," Elizabeth added.

"Good. I'm glad she did." William smiled at his princess, took her hand and kissed it before going on with his story. "After they were pronounced husband and wife, Richard told her she could go by any name she wanted. She told him, and everyone else, that she would be 'Richard's Wife' from that moment on. And for some reason, we just refer to her that way. It always makes her smile. Seems to stroke Rich's ego as well."

"I think it's sweet. Confused the hell out of me, but it is endearing."

"Good. Now tell me why would your sister name her daughter after a brand of orange juice?" William asked, and Elizabeth rolled her eyes.

❧ ❧ ❧

"Will is going to take you on a Caribbean cruise? For holiday?" Georgiana said with her hands on her hips. "He never took me on a cruise!"

"Why would I take my younger sister on a cruise?" William interjected.

"Why not?" Georgiana snipped.

"Couples go on cruises, dear sister, so they can ...."

"Don't you dare say it. Ew! Ew! Ew!" Georgiana practically ran out of the room.

"That was mean." Elizabeth said with a smile.

"Like I would want to take my little sister on a romantic cruise."

"Ah, but you will take the woman you are sleeping with," Elizabeth said as she pressed herself up against him.

"You did say that you would marry me after all. I figure that deserves a reward of some sort."

"I thought you were supposed to be my reward?"

"Well, I am, but I thought I would toss in something extra."

"You are such a nice man," Elizabeth said as just before she pressed her lips to William's.

"I thought we could fly to New York and do some shopping first."

"Shopping? William Darcy, have you lost your senses? You don't shop!"

"I do with you, Princess. Besides, according to the brochure, there is a black-and-white ball on board. You'll need a white and very formal dress to go with my black tux."

"If you say so, but I don't think it's necessary."

"Humor me," William whispered before he took her mouth with his.

❧ ❧ ❧

William loaded up all their luggage and latest purchases into the trunk of the rented car, then opened the door for Elizabeth and helped her in.

"I don't know why you want to drive all the way from New York to Miami. We could just as well fly."

"I know, but we've done all our shopping, and there is still a week before the ship sails. I thought it would be nice to drive and see the countryside. I haven't been here in years, love. Besides, the lake is on the way. Wouldn't it be nice to see if the cave is still there?"

"Will, I wonder about you sometimes."

"No you don't. Even if you did, you would just have a vision telling you what I'm about," William smiled. He was fascinated with Elizabeth's ability, and he tried to help her accept that it was normal for her to have visions. She had told him of her wanting to hide her ability, not let anyone know and how and why she would doubt what she would see, even though every vision had manifested. Well, except one.

"Ha, ha, very funny, Mr. Darcy."

"Lizzy?" William asked as he drove along the interstate.

"Hmm?"

"I was wondering."

"Uh huh?" Elizabeth replied as she looked through a magazine.

"Will you marry me?"

Elizabeth looked over at William. "I believe I already answered that question. Do think I'm going to run off or something, Will? I'm not, you know."

"I know. I meant, will you marry me today?"

"Today?"

"Yes. At the lake... in the woods... at our cave?"

Elizabeth couldn't hold back her tears. She swiped at them as she nodded her reply.

"You can wear that while gown you chose for the ball..."

"And I have just the shoes for it! But..." Elizabeth's joy seemed to slip.

"What is it, honey?"

"My family, friends, Georgiana..."

"This is for us. We will do something with them as well. But this is for us."

Elizabeth smiled again and nodded.

Everything had been arranged days before, and Elizabeth couldn't have been more surprised and thrilled with William's romantic surprise. It was perfect. It was how they started, so it was only natural it was how they should begin the next part of their lives.

Elizabeth dressed in the white gown she found in New York and added the ballerina shoes. The lady who ran the lake retreat placed a tiara she had left over from a costume party on top of Elizabeth's veil to keep the breeze from blowing it off into the trees during the ceremony.

Elizabeth walked slowly through the trees and to her knight, who stood guard just outside the small cave. After taking their vows and kissing to seal the bond, William and Elizabeth Darcy walked slowly to the main cabin, where they would share a bit of cake and some Champagne.

"I love you, Elizabeth," William whispered in her ear. "I hope you like your present."

Elizabeth looked at William with an odd glance just before he pushed the door to the main cabin open. The sudden sound of applause jolted her as she realized her entire family, all of her friends, Georgiana and Richard and Caroline all stood inside.

"Dangnab you, Elizabeth!" Elizabeth turned to see Jane growl at her then stomp her foot! "How dare you run off and get married like that!"

Elizabeth stared at her sister.

"It was the most beautiful thing I ever saw!" Jane pointed to the big screen television on the far wall. "The whole thing was being filmed, and we watched in here as it happened."

Elizabeth didn't seem to register the television or the fact that her wedding had been televised to all in the clubhouse.

"Lizzy! Lizzy!" Sara Gardiner shouted as she ran up to her older cousin. "You're so pretty. You look like a princess!"

Elizabeth turned to her new husband and said, "You made it come true! This is what I saw... in the cave... all those years ago!"

William Darcy smiled. "I love you, Princess!"

Epilogue

"It's been a long time since we've been here," Elizabeth whispered as her husband, behind her, wrapped his arms about her waist.

"Our wedding day," William said softly into her ear before he kissed her neck, just below her lobe.

"It's a beautiful night. The sky is clear and the stars are flooding the sky." Elizabeth stroked her husband's cheek as she spoke.

"And all the kids are asleep."

"How many stories did you have to read Elsa to get her down?"

"Four, but she liked the one I told her about the knight who found a princess in a cave."

"Mr. Darcy! Are you telling your children fairytales again?"

"Oh, quite the contrary, Mrs. Darcy!" William turned his wife to face him then proceeded to kiss her senseless. "Besides, Elsa looks so much like her mum, that it's hard to refuse her."

"Yeah, she has you completely wrapped around her little finger!" Elizabeth laughed.

"Are you saying that my children control me?"

"Well, let's just say that you can be a very indulgent father, but I think Elsa has the most power over you," Elizabeth spoke with a gleam in her eye.

"She's only four, Lizzy! And perhaps a bit too much like her mother!"

"Are you trying to say that I have power over you?" Elizabeth caressed the back of Will's neck as she asked her question.

William growled and pulled her hard against his body. Suddenly he pulled away and grabbed her hand and said, "Come with me, woman!"

"Ooo, what a caveman!"

"More than you know. Your parents are going to stay with the kids. You, my dear wife, are coming with me!"

William escorted Elizabeth away from the large cabin that held his family for the special Darcy Corp. retreat to honor Thomas Bennet's thirty-five years with the company. They took a path that led into the woods. William wrapped his arm around Elizabeth's body and held her close to his side as they trekked through trees.

"You're taking me to the cave!" Elizabeth exclaimed with a smile.

"Of course, where else would a caveman take the woman he loves?"

"Oh, let's see... Well, I believe I recall you playing caveman in the garage after we came home from our honeymoon cruise..."

"Hmmm, yes. I do believe that is how we ended up with Thomas," William commented and Elizabeth laughed.

"Then there was that time in that closet at the hospital when Caroline and Richard's second child was born."

"I still say that's where we made Stephanie."

"I disagree, Will. I think it was when we drove up to Derbyshire."

"At least we can agree on how ended up with Daniel, Patrice and Elsa," William smiled as he spoke his children's names.

"I do believe you like making babies, my adorable caveman!"

"I do and I want to make another one in our cave, Lizzy." William took her mouth in a searing kiss and backed her up into the cave where their lives together first started.

❦ ❦ ❦

"I do think it was sweet of William to throw such an elaborate party in honor of your retirement, dear," Fanny Bennet said as she pulled out her knitting.

"He really did go to too much trouble, but I must admit I am enjoying this," Thomas Bennet said as he put his feet up in the Darcy cabin. "Besides allowing me a job that I loved for years, the man has given me five grandchildren in ten years."

"Grandchildren you almost humiliated him into not giving you!"

"Fanny! He was seventeen! Lizzy was twelve. They weren't ready! Besides we talked about that years ago. When George died and I went to England for the funeral, Will and I talked all that out. You know that. It would have been difficult for us to work together otherwise. It was embarrassing for us both, but we managed to come to an understanding." Tom watched his wife work her knitting needles as he spoke. "What are you working on?"

"Oh, just a pair of booties and a matching hat," Mrs. Bennet answered.

"Blue. Someone is having a boy?"

"Yes," Fanny looked at her husband and smiled.

"Not you!"

"Oh, for goodness sake, Thomas Bennet! I'm a bit old for that! Well, old for having a child at any rate. Though it is a surprise."

"Oh, who is going to be surprised? Charles? I know he and Jane have been trying for another one."

"No. Not Jane and Charles, Thomas. How quickly you forget."

"Ah, My Lizzy and Will!"

"Yes," Mrs. Bennet smiled. "But remember, we aren't supposed to know. Lizzy wanted us to sit with kids so she could tell him."

"I think they went to the cave," Mr. Bennet smiled.

"Of course they did, Thomas."

❦ ❦ ❦

William and Elizabeth held each other close. A soft summer breeze drifted into the cave and cooled their sweat-dampened nude forms.

"Do you think we made another little one tonight, Lizzy?" William said in a contented voice.

"I don't think so," she answered happily.

"Don't you want another baby, Lizzy?" William asked, slightly concerned at the mix of her happiness and her answer.

"William Darcy! I told you that I wanted to have a hundred children with you if it were possible. But I know we didn't make a baby tonight because we made one about six weeks ago!" She smiled broadly at him.

As her words finally registered, he smiled broadly and kissed her over and over until they made love again to celebrate adding to their family.

❦ ❦ ❦

Almost eight months later...

"Tommy, Steph, Danny, Tricie and Elsa, meet your new baby brother," Elizabeth said as she sat in a rocker in her hospital room.

"Good! Another boy!" Ten year-old Tommy exclaimed. "Now we're even!"

"I'm prettier than he is," Elsa stated as she looked at the sleeping baby, unimpressed.

"May I help take care of him, Mum?" Stephanie asked. "I'm almost nine, so I'm very responsible."

"How long before he can play footie?" asked the serious seven year-old Danny, a carbon copy of his father in appearance.

Patrice carefully approached and studied the baby. The girl seemed to be a miniature adult instead of the five-year-old she was. "He's bald. He better grow some hair fast, because I don't think anyone will be impressed otherwise."

William Darcy couldn't help but smirk at his little girl's grown up vocabulary; she was going to be a scholar one day, he just knew it!

"Yes, well... we are even now. Three boys, three girls, and of course you are prettier that he is, Elsa. You are a girl!" He bent down and kissed the top of the young girl's head. "I think your Mum would appreciate some help, Stephanie."

"I would," Elizabeth agreed with her husband as she watched him herd his children toward the door.

"Danny, I think it will be a few years before your new brother will be playing footie, but I'm sure he will love it if you teach him. And Patrice, I wouldn't worry about his hair. I believe you were also bald, and see what beautiful hair you have now?"

Elizabeth rocked her new son and waited for her husband to return and escort her out so they could go home as a family.

"Are you ready, Princess?" William Darcy looked at his wife with a glimmer in his eye.

"I am, Sir William of Darcy, my dashing knight!"

"And what about my new son?"

"Master Clifford Robert Darcy is ready too, love."

~ fini ~

3602203

Made in the USA